A ROMANTIC COMEDY

A ROMANTIC COMEDY

SUSAN SURMAN

PROSPECTIVE PRESS
Winston-Salem

PROSPECTIVE PRESS LLC

1959 Peace Haven Rd, #246, Winston-Salem, NC 27106 U.S.A.
www.prospectivepress.com

Published in the United States of America by PROSPECTIVE PRESS LLC

TRADEMARK

WEST PALM GIG

Author photo by Linda Weaver

Interior design by ARTE RAVE

ISBN 978-1-943419-21-0

First PROSPECTIVE PRESS trade paperback edition

Printed in the United States of America
First printing, August, 2016

1 3 5 7 9 10 8 6 4 2

The text of this book was typeset in Minion Pro
Accent text was typeset in Blakely

Previously published in 2012 under the same title by a different publisher.
The text has been revised and expanded for this new edition.

CAST OF CHARACTERS

VALESKA BERNHART	Hollywood film star makes a last stab at a movie role at an open casting call before retiring to West Palm Acres where she learns talent doesn't have an expiration date.
GLICK GLICKMAN	Fast talking, multi-faceted theatre impresario, hoping to revive the dead Broadway theatre with his Revue before retiring to West Palm Acres where he learns artists never retire.
JON SULLIVAN	Out-of-work New York actor hired to remind the residents at West Palm Acres to take their medication. In the process, he discovers who he really wants to be.
HARRY GOLDBERG	Know-it-all resident at West Palm Acres. Mad about the movies and movie stars. Shares an apartment with Oscar.
OSCAR SHAPIRO	Star-struck resident at West Palm Acres. Harry's roommate.
TARA BOMBECK	Multi-pierced and tattooed independent filmmaker casting her first, low-budget film.
JANE SMITH	Plain, clumsy assistant to Glick Glickman, secretly in love with him, until a telegram reveals her true identity.
ROCKY RAGE	Fat and funny actor. Always hungry. In love with Ruby. A member of Glick's theatrical Company.
INKY KRABB	Skinny, nervous, funny actress. In love with Rocky. A member of Glick's theatrical Company.
RUBY VALK	Glamorous leading lady. In love with Enzo. A member of Glick's theatrical Company.
ENZO BORDELLO	Handsome leading man. In love with himself. A member of Glick's theatrical Company.
FAT CAT	A sleazy ex-con brought in at the final hour as a potential backer for Glick's Revue. Origins unknown.

1

CLOWN SULLIVAN

Dead clown walking, he thought, tongue in cheek, even though it *was* an apt title for his current circumstances. At least he hadn't lost his sense of humor. Here he was, Jon Sullivan, an established, New York-based actor, walking up and down the hallways of one of Florida's premier retirement communities, situated in West Palm Beach, reminding residents to take their pills. Yes! At periodical intervals reminding residents to take their pills. And getting paid for it! And he was dressed in a clown costume. A clown costume! In between acting jobs, actors often took odd jobs. Nothing could be odder than this one.

He was ageless in the clown suit, not that that was the intention. As it happened, he was thirty-four, had an acting range of four or five years either way, was tall, and he was single. Two years ago, he had taken a job on a cruise ship and was part of a troupe doing their thing on the high seas nightly. His specialty was a juggling act and telling a few jokes at the same time. Not a very good sailor, he had spent most of his off-stage hours in the head of his tiny quarters. He vowed no matter how bad things got, no matter how long he had to wait for an acting role, he was never going to do a cruise ship thing again.

There was that word. Never. A word never to be used.

Under the clown costume, which was a little warm on his body, but nothing unbearable, Jon's appearance was fairly generic, a fairly average Joe type guy. Except for his hair. His hair was red. In bright sunlight, it looked orange. In Florida, he looked like he was sporting a bright red tomato on his head. He had lovely soft brown eyes and once people got over the hair the eyes are what they focused on. Growing up, he was teased in the neighborhood because no one had hair like that. His mother didn't have red-orange hair, his father didn't have red-orange hair, his sister had a nice head of brown hair. His mother's, "That's how it happens sometimes," was explanation enough and couldn't be questioned. Jon grew up and outgrew hating being a redhead. By college, they were calling him 'Red' after Red Skelton, who was his hero. And when his career was beginning to take off, he was easily identifiable in the acting game by producers and directors when he went to auditions. "Let's get the redhead" or "Call back the redhead for a second reading" or "Who's the redhead's agent?" It was his calling card. And he wasn't going to fight it. And besides, depending on the role, the color could always be dyed.

He didn't mind being a bachelor. It allowed him to be able to gallivant around freely, taking jobs where they came up. It wasn't that he was anti-women. Hardly. He dated lots of actresses, but nothing ever developed into a serious relationship; that is, he got out before it got to that next level, much to the disappointment of his parents and probably the female party. He never stayed around long enough to find out. He wasn't a cad or anything like that. It's just that he believed when a thing was over, it was over. No need to conduct a post-mortem.

His parents still lived in the same house where he was born, just outside Chicago. They thought their son was in

New York teaching a course called "Creativity in Communication" at a city college. It was easier to let them think so. The ultra-conservative Sullivans never would have understood or approved of his lifestyle. Actually, he had taught an acting class one semester, so it was more of a fib than an out-and-out lie. The real lie was about his name change. His birth name was Duane Sullivan, Junior, but thinking it would be easier to say, spell, and remember, he had changed it to Jon when he moved to the big Apple fourteen years ago. Jon told his family there were too many Duane Sullivans in New York, especially in communication. Trusting souls, they never doubted his choice.

He had had to reveal many of these details in an interview before West Palm Acres would hire him. He had also been subjected to a drug test. He didn't even drink wine, never had, and never had the desire to snort anything. When his urine test came out a copper color, he was suspected of something, but the lab technicians couldn't put their finger on it. A second test proved him to be safe. Further investigation revealed that the copper color was attributed to the fact that Jon had eaten about half a pound of red beets the night before the test.

Auditioning for a Broadway show or a television role was less intensive than this audition at West Palm Acres, but he needed money, so he didn't complain. In a way, it was kind of an acting job. He was in costume. He was playing a character. He had to knock on doors and remind residents to take their pills. He had received a script to memorize his one line. He had been given directions. Definitely an acting role.

He was now in the fourth floor hallway, labeled the penthouse by the residents, of Building G at West Palm Acres. He checked his clipboard with the list of apartments and residents. 4-G was next. The brass nameplate was etched with the names **Harry Goldberg** and **Oscar Shapiro**.

Jon took a deep breath and called out, "Mister Goldberg, it's time to take your pill!" Getting no response, Jon knocked on the dark green steel door. Not so much a knock knock, but rather a light rap. Still getting no response, he banged three times with a closed fist before shouting out the next directive. "Mister Shapiro, it's time to take your pill!" Jon waited. Pressing the bell would have been easier, but it was an absolute last resort. Something to do with the shrill sound of the buzzer startling the folks with sensitive ears; maybe faulty hearing aids. A hand knock, then the brass knocker only if necessary. No bell. He didn't question the direction. Per his theatrical training, he did as he was told.

He waited. Sometimes it took a resident a little time to answer the door. So far, his first day on the job at the place was going satisfactorily. Actually, he didn't know if it was going satisfactorily or not, never having been a medical clown before. No one in management knew if it was going well or not. The launch of a new experiment to remind residents to take their medications would take time to assess. Medical clown. He let out a snort. Oh, well, just another role, but one he would leave off his bio.

While waiting for Goldberg and Shapiro to appear, he studied the décor which had a dizzying effect; repelling, yet strangely attractive. It was the same on all the floors. The walls were papered in floral prints of bright shades of emerald green, orange, yellow, and varying shades of purple to blend in, more or less, with the varied color of the doors. The floors were covered in a thin carpet of a pattern in corresponding colors. Only in Florida. Jon learned along the way that the wallpaper would soon be replaced by a simpler pattern of swaying palm trees on a white background. Nice. He also learned this was a rumor started and spread around for many years by a longstanding resident on the second floor.

It had taken nearly four hours to get around the seven buildings on the property all with the similar design: four floors, each with an elevator, thirty apartments. About eighty percent were two bedrooms; the other twenty percent were made up of studios and one bedroom. This information he learned from the brochure at his training session. He didn't actually go around and count. Jon welcomed the exercise. After a short break, he started the rounds again. That way, everyone was reminded to take their pills at what had been deemed the general interval between prescribed medications. No one had worked through what happened if a resident was not in his apartment when the knock came from Sullivan. There were multiple activities going on all the time at West Palm Acres from arts and crafts classes to the musical group called Flats and Sharps to the aquatics at the heated indoor and outdoor pools, yoga classes, card games, and tables with complicated looking puzzles. Anyway, it was early days, so no one was worried about flaws yet. The general consensus was that the kinks would get worked out in the doing. That's why it was called an experiment.

Jon's voice projection was good as he reminded each resident on his list about their pills. Too bad his voice projection hadn't helped him get an acting job in nearly eight months. And before that, there was a long interval between acting jobs. Between jobs, actors waited for the magic call from their agents about the next job. When this gig came up, he had no choice but to accept. He had hated leaving all the action in New York, but he'd hung around long enough with nothing happening and when you need work, you go where the work is, whatever it is. He figured a job out of the acting business would be less of a stigma if he was out of town, away from the mainstream of the highly competitive acting community. And winter was rolling in up north, so he wasn't going to mind being warm for a while. The job included bed and board and a small stipend, enough to cover his rent controlled studio apartment in a pretty good neighborhood in lower Manhattan.

Signs of life behind the door to 4-G finally could be heard, and Jon Sullivan had something to focus on other than Jon Sullivan. Typical of many actors, he was always going over his credentials; if not actually citing them to anyone, rehearsing them in his mind to reinforce his abilities in case he had to cite them to anyone. It was just one of the many idiosyncrasies of an actor.

Two short men stood in the now opened doorway looking up at the gigantic stranger. The man on the right snapped, "If you're from the travel people, we already told them we don't want to do the day trip on the cruise ship."

The man on the left explained to Jon, who didn't know which one was Goldberg and which one was Shapiro, "Everyone goes so they can gamble for the day. I get seasick at the indoor pool we got here, never mind an ocean voyage. It's heated, the indoor pool. Also the outdoor pool. Heated all year round. I still get sick."

"Another country heard from," the other one said. "Besides, it isn't a voyage, dummy." To Jon, he explained, "The ship stands still for fifteen hours, maybe five. It doesn't go anywhere. So are you the one yelling about some cockamamie pills?" And looking him up and down, he added, "In a clown get-up yet. Or maybe your everyday attire? I hope they don't add an entertainment tax to my monthly tab."

Jon couldn't tell if this was humor or disdain. After all, a stranger in a clown costume telling you to take your pill could create some mistrust. With the door open, Jon glimpsed how dark it was in the apartment.

One of the gentlemen picked up on Jon's look and volunteered an explanation. "The sun's so bright, we can't see the TV, so we keep the blinds closed."

"Too much sun is bad for the complexion they're saying now," the other one said.

It was necessary to get down to business. Looking down at the little man on the right, Jon said in a serious tone, "It's time to take your pill, Mister Goldberg." Little as in height, not meaning a person of lesser value.

Without hesitation, the man said with authority, "I'm Shapiro. The ugly one is Goldberg." The arthritic finger first pointed then poked his roommate in the ribs.

Ignoring the ugly reference, the pointed finger, and the poke, Goldberg restored himself. "We took the pill ten minutes ago," he said with authority. "Since we have the same prescription approximately, we split it in half. Saves on the medical expenses. And health-wise, we feel the same with or without the pill; with or without the whole or the half." Nodding towards Shapiro, he said matter-of-factly, "If he dies, he dies."

Jon had trouble believing the explanation about their creative pill taking. Apart from not believing them, he wasn't sure if what they said they did was even legal or medically correct; but, as he was only supposed to deliver the one line giving them the reminder to take the pill and not monitor the actual taking of it, he said nothing.

Harry Goldberg caught sight of the elevator door opening down the hall. Without moving, he called out to no one, "Somebody hold the damn door. I gotta eat." To the clown, he emphasized, "Whoever heard of a dining room in a basement? My relationship with food while facing a damn brick wall."

Oscar Shapiro quickly added, no doubt to impress the clown, "Don't listen to him. It's not a basement. It's the first floor. There's a big palm tree out there in a beautiful garden with a white stone bench."

"Don't listen to him. It's a basement. I'm paying monthly

fees for an underground garden with a brick wall," Harry Goldberg said, adding, "The bench is gray."

"We're thinking of getting a petition up to change the name West Palm Acres to Garden of the Moon," Oscar Shapiro said. "It has a romantic touch. Garden of the Moon."

"Romance, shmomance. It'll never happen." Turning his attention to the clown, Harry Goldberg said, "There was a movie where that doctor character put on a clown face to make the kid patients feel better. Are you a medical person?"

"Doctor. You mean, doctor," corrected Oscar Shapiro.

"What?" asked Goldberg.

"Doctor. Not medical person," Shapiro corrected impatiently. That's what you said."

"What's the matter with you? That's what I said."

Not wanting to get in the middle of their thing, whatever their thing was, Jon jumped in. "Look guys, I'm just a kind of aide in a clown suit. I've been hired to go floor to floor, door to door, up and down to all the apartments in all the buildings. That way, everyone gets a nice reminder every four to five hours to take the next pill. It's a new experiment. Management thought the clown suit would add a bit of fun for the patients. I mean residents." He quickly made the correction, but it was too late. The grave error had already slipped from his lips. To take their minds off his stupid fluff, in a stage voice from his lower register, he proudly announced, "In real life, I'm an actor. My name is Jon Sullivan, without the 'h'. You may have seen me in some things." He held out his hand, not to be kissed, but perhaps to be shaken as a goodwill gesture.

Ignoring the extended white gloved hand of the clown, Goldberg and Shapiro looked at one another before looking back up at the clown. *Actor?* They'd been injected in the arm with a life-enhancing serum just by the word. They loved actors, acting, anything to do with performers, stars, television, movies. All of it. Just the name *Hollywood* gave them a buzz.

"I saw you on the box last night," Goldberg announced, shaking his head with approval. "You're very good."

"No you didn't, moron," Shapiro reprimanded. To Jon, he said, "Don't listen to him, Clown Solomon."

At first, Jon wasn't sure he should make the correction, but in the end, he did. "Sullivan. Jon. You don't have to say the clown part. Just Jon Sullivan." It didn't matter. No one was listening.

Shapiro explained, "Listen, last night, we attended a program in the auditorium on reversing arteries, so my roommate here couldn't have seen you."

"Heart disease," Goldberg corrected. "Not reversing. It was about arteries. How can you reverse arteries? And besides, it wasn't reversing. It was the other re word." He thought a second before coming up with, "Reconstructing." The attempt to snap his fingers didn't quite work. He tried again. Still no luck. He gave up.

"What are you talking about?" Shapiro said sharply. Turning away from Goldberg, he addressed the clown in a softer tone. "We see movies now and again, but they are nothing like they used to be. We used to see every movie that was ever made. In a real movie theater. Big screen. Lots of seats. Down and up. A balcony." His eyes shone as he recalled the time. "Maybe we've seen you; maybe not."

Caught up in the reverie of the bygone movie days, Goldberg said, "Back then, they showed a movie, then a live orchestra came right up out of the floor, then a second movie. Remember, Oscar? Harry James. Benny Goodman. Tommy Dorsey. That was a real show."

"Remember!" exclaimed Shapiro. "I was there! Twenty-five cents every Saturday. It was a lot of money back then.

We weren't rich, but we always found the money to go to the movies."

"Every Saturday, we were there." Goldberg eyes misted as he remembered.

"So you guys knew one another a long time ago." Jon meant it as a question, but it came out like a statement.

"Are you kidding? Over fifty years I know this *ganef*," said Shapiro with affection.

"Once I borrowed a button from him, so I became a *ganef*, a crook, according to him," Goldberg said with equal affection. "*Ganef* he thinks sounds more classy so he uses it. We worked together in the garment district on Seventh Avenue in New York," he explained. The images raced through his brain and just for that moment in time, you could see the switch on his face and he wasn't here but there.

"Manhattan," Shapiro corrected.

Ignoring him, Goldberg went on. "It was a time when clothes had really good stitching. We were tailors," he said with great pride. He reached out and touched the front of the loose jacket Jon had on. "Excuse me, do you mind?"

Jon gave the go ahead nod.

Harry handled a button. He lifted up the collar and ran his finger down a seam. "*Oi.* Look at this, Oscar. Machine. Today, they don't know one stitch from another. He'll be lucky if this outfit lasts through the week. Three days tops."

"They did that because of the heat. Had to make it lightweight. It's just a costume," Jon mumbled, straightening his collar and heeding their words without tugging too heavily on the fabric. He said brightly, "I bet those were the days, huh? Anyone who was anyone wore hand-tailored."

Shapiro was thinking movies, not shirts. "Do you know the actress Sharon Stone? Some beauty."

"What about Rosalind Russell? Ever meet her?" Goldberg piped in, adding, "Jewish. A lot of people didn't know that." This type of conversation made him tingle with excitement.

"They didn't know that because she wasn't Jewish," Shapiro snapped.

"What are you talking about, moron? She was Jewish. Real name was Goldberg."

"That's your name, dummy."

"We were distant cousins."

"I know you fifty-three years. How come I never knew that?"

"I don't tell you everything."

"Why not?"

Jon was enjoying the two, but he couldn't allow himself to be drawn into their debate because with this pill job, time was of the essence. He excused himself and headed down the hallway to the next door, a little surprised, but not sorry, that the vaudeville team was following. At their own pace, of course.

4-H. The place where the name should be was blank. He checked the list on his clipboard notes. Hank Herman, 4-H. Jon put his ear to the door. Not hearing anything, he shouted, "Mister Herman, it's time to take your pill!" Jon waited a couple of seconds. He knocked on the lime green steel door. "Mister Herman?"

When the duo of Goldberg and Shapiro caught up to him, in unison they announced in flat tones, "He's dead."

"Dropped right into the soup. Only eighty-three. A kid," said the eighty-seven year old Harry Goldberg. "Three days ago in the dining room in the middle of lunch. Just like that." Another attempt to snap his fingers didn't work.

Out of respect, Shapiro lowered his head before speaking. "We don't know who's moving in. It's a nice big unit. Two bedrooms, two bathrooms, make-shift kitchen. Just like ours. We don't cook. I'm eighty-seven."

"Eighty-nine," Goldberg corrected. "I'm eighty seven."

"Are you sure?" Shapiro tried to do a mental calculation, but gave up "Oh, well, it's only a number."

"Until you have to get out of bed in the morning." Goldberg never talked about it to strangers, but his hips, knees, feet, eyelids, ears, elbows, and fingers ached constantly.

It was back to the movies with Harry and Oscar continuing their observations about who was and who was not Jewish in Hollywood.

Jon crossed Hank Herman's name off his list. "Weren't you guys going down to the dining room?" Jon asked concerned they might be missing their meal time.

"I'm not hungry," Shapiro said.

"They want us to eat lunch at nine-thirty in the morning," grumbled Goldberg.

"And dinner at four in the afternoon. The *verkakte* early bird special," complained Shapiro. "I used to eat a big lunch when I was young around one o'clock. Then dinner, only then they called it supper, was at seven, eight; sometimes as late as eight-thirty."

"You mean when you could chew," said Goldberg.

Ignoring the person he shared his living accommodations with, he said, "I don't know what I'm supposed to eat when."

"Or when to eat what," added Goldberg. "Mind you, the mashed yams yesterday weren't too bad."

"Too dry," said Shapiro. "Now they call them sweet potatoes, I think."

"Same thing."

"Sunday was the day we had chicken with yam potatoes."

"Yam is a potato. You don't have to say yam potato," corrected Goldberg.

Oscar Shapiro was strolling down memory lane and wasn't listening to Harry. "My mother worked full time so the kitchen was my grandmother's department. We all lived together. Roast chicken for lunch, a chicken sandwich with lettuce and mayonnaise on toasted white bread for dinner while I listened to my favorite programs on the radio. Jack Benny. Fred Allen. Amos 'n Andy. On Monday, my grandmother sent me to school with a thick sliced chicken sandwich on thick white bread and Monday night, we had chicken salad with chopped celery on a bed of lettuce. In those days, no one worried about allergies and arthritis and inflamed joints. Why would that matter when there was the wishbone ritual? The wishbone. The highlight. Every Sunday, my grandmother would pull it off the cooked chicken, dry it off with a paper towel and hold it out to me. I grabbed one end in my small hand while she held the other end and we each made a wish. Then we pulled the bones apart. The one who got the fat end was the winner. That person's wish would come true. I can't remember what I wished for."

"Probably for a more varied menu," chuckled Goldberg.

Jon wasn't sure where this bantering was headed or if it had come to an end, so he excused himself and walked down the hall to the next door. The duo was right behind him.

4-J was a purple door and the brass plate was marked **Valeska Bernhart**. He was puzzled. He looked at his list. Had he missed a door?

Reading his mind, Shapiro volunteered, "The 'I' is eliminated at West Palm Acres. No one knows why."

"No one cares," added Goldberg.

Checking that the nameplate matched the name on his clipboard, Jon knocked on the door and then called out, "Missuz Bernhart, it's time to take your pill." Valeska Bernhart, Valeska Bernhart. It couldn't be. Just a coincidence. Still…with such an unusual name, there couldn't be two, could there? He'd soon find out.

Goldberg and Shapiro immediately shifted their focus. The sound of Missuz rang out a different tune to them. Stretching their five feet five and a half inch frames as tall as they could, they looked up at the brass nameplate on the door. **Valeska Bernhart.**

"I told you a new woman moved in, Oscar. They made the floor co-ed." Goldberg knew he had never told him, because he didn't know any such thing, but in every group, there is always the one who liked everyone to think he was the one with the inside information. In this group, that person was Goldberg.

"What are you so excited for, Harry? Valeska could be a man's name," Oscar said.

Harry studied the name. His eyes narrowed. "You know who this is? This is Valeska Bernhart." He let his brain wrap around that thought. "But it can't be. On the other hand, it isn't a name like every Tom, Dick, and Harry. How many people could have the same name? And if it is, in which case as it happens, it would be Miss. You know they go by their maiden names in show business."

"What are you talking about?" And then as quickly as the words had come out of his mouth, the penny dropped. Shapiro recognized the name, too. "You think it could be? Sooner or later we all end up in a home like this, so why not her? And why not here?" He had high hopes.

Harry Goldberg took great umbrage at the home reference. "Excuse me. West Palm Acres is a very upscale classy retirement community; not, as you say, a home. Otherwise, I wouldn't be here."

"This could be my lucky day." The white skin on Oscar's face turned a light pink.

"Your lucky day? You? Oscar Shapiro? Why would she look at you? For chrissakes, she danced with Valentino!"

"You're crazy. That would make her two hundred years old."

"On screen, they do things to make them look younger."

"How do you know that?"

"*The Doctors*. It's a medical program on TV."

As far as co-ed, there was no such differential at West Palm Acres. The apartments housed a mixed population with the widows outnumbering the widowers about four to one. There was also the smattering of elderly married couples and a few folks who had hooked up since arriving at the place, but permanent co-habitation of these unmarried couples was strictly forbidden. While they might eat together in the dining room and sit next to one another on bus trips, and traipse down the hall when everyone else was asleep for nightly visits, living in a permanent situation together was frowned upon. The reason was obvious. It was strictly economical. Business is business. Why lease only one apartment, when you could get money on two apartments?

Harry Goldberg brushed a hand down the side of his nearly bald head, a reflex reaction, no doubt in reverence to his once thick dark brown hair that had turned to salt and pepper before losing the battle and finally revealing his bullet-shaped dome. He carefully adjusted his heavily framed bifocals. Only those closest to him knew that even with the thick glasses, he had to use a magnifying glass to read the newspaper. "How do I look?" he asked Oscar.

Looking him up and down, knowing what Harry was really thinking, Oscar was grateful that he still could boast nearly a full head of white hair. He replied with as much diplomacy as he could muster, not wanting to be mean, not wanting to lie, not wanting to tell the truth, "Like you always look."

And this satisfied Harry.

Oscar didn't want to get his hopes up that this was really *the* Valeska Bernhart. Nevertheless, he carefully adjusted his recently acquired rimless progressive eyeglasses without the obvious bi-focal line that he was sure made him look younger. While Goldberg may have had the personality, he definitely had the looks.

"She must have moved in yesterday," Harry said. He pulled back his shoulders and puffed out his chest in an attempt to look vertical. It only made him more horizontal.

At last, the door to 4-J opened slowly. The occupant, a woman indeed, looked at the trio of two old men and a clown. At five feet three inches tall, with hair so black it looked like a crow sitting on her head, with a face painted with black eyeliner, pink rouge, and bright red lipstick, Valeska Bernhart resembled an old-fashioned kewpie doll. Goldberg and Shapiro felt like giants. At five feet eleven and a half, Jon, the actor/aide in the clown suit, wasn't sure how he felt.

Oscar broke the silence. "May we accompany you to the dining room, Miz Bernhart?" He was sure his voice was self-assured and rather young sounding.

"We have a good table by the kitchen, *Miss* Bernhart. The food stays hot," lied Harry.

"By the kitchen, the food stays hot," repeated Shapiro. No need to mention it was the worst seating arrangement in the dining room. If you had the seat with your back to the kitchen, every time someone came out with a tray, you risked getting bopped in the head with either the swinging door or the tray.

"I just said that. The food stays hot, Miss Bernhart," said Goldberg.

For Oscar, there was no one here now but Oscar Shapiro and Valeska Bernhart. "Take my arm, Miz Bernhart." He extended his good arm out to her.

"Take your pill, Miss Bernhart," Jon said. This really was Valeska Bernhart. Everyone who was in the business knew who she was. She was hot for a very long time, then nothing.

A few years back, he'd seen a documentary about the film stars of yesteryear. She did some things on Broadway, too. She was great. Maybe she could give him some introductions. Then he remembered his position and why he was here. It wasn't to ogle old time film stars. It was about medication. He wasn't sure whether she had taken her pill or not. Again, he reminded her.

A clown telling her to take her pill didn't seem unusual to Valeska Bernhart who had just arrived from California at the insistence of her daughter who lived in Florida. To her alleged suitors, she said, "I have to take the pill with food. Wait while I get my cane. I'll go with you to the dining room." The cane was new. It was all new.

To Goldberg and Shapiro, her distinctive Metro Goldwyn Mayer major studio accent and tone sounded like sweet butter melting in the center of a freshly baked, warm bran and raisin muffin, which regrettably was taboo on their respective diets.

Jon hadn't seen anyone take their pills. His training had included knocking on the doors and shouting out the instructions. The rules hadn't specified actually supervising them swallowing the pills. He didn't think that would even be ethical. He wasn't a doctor. He had never even played a doctor. He would just have to trust that they were following their regime. Anxious to stick to his time-table, leaving the newly formed trio behind, he moved down the hall to the next door.

4-K. **Arnold Solloway** was the name on the brass plate. Jon rapped on the tangerine colored steel door and shouted, "Mister Solloway, it's time to take your pill!" He waited. Again, he called out, "Mister Solloway, it's time to take your pill!" He listened for movement inside. It was quiet. Too quiet. He didn't like the feeling he was getting. He turned the knob. The door opened. First, he peered around the door and then went in slowly so as not to alarm the resident who may only be hard of hearing.

A man Jon assumed to be Arnold Solloway appeared to be asleep in the armchair in the living room. A distinct musty odor wafted up from the faded neutral wall-to-wall carpet that covered the floor throughout, except for the kitchenette against the wall. There, there was a small stretch of light tan linoleum. A bedroom was in plain sight. It looked like the bed had been slept in but not made up. A smattering of tables and chairs from a bygone era gave the whole space a rather depressing atmosphere. Jon gently nudged the shoulder of the man who was slumped over in his chair. "Mister Solloway, it's time to take your pill." He said it close to the man's ear in just a bit above a whisper. But Jon knew his words were useless.

Jon had played a cop once on a TV show and his character was the one who discovered the dead man in his hotel room. And he had read enough crime novels to know dead when he saw dead. He lingered, unafraid, untouched by being in the same room with the body. As a trained actor, he couldn't help try to figure out the back story. Who was Arnold Solloway? What was his life? Where was he from? Was there any family? He stood over the dead man in the threadbare chair and stared at him for a few minutes before reaching into his pocket for the pager that had been issued to him by the office in case of an emergency. This was definitely one of those. He punched in the code, explained the situation, was thanked by the staff member on the other end, and told it wasn't necessary to wait in the apartment. It can happen that quickly. Arnold Solloway was fine early that morning when he was checked on, one of the features of West Palm Acres, not that they put that fact in the brochure. They preferred their residents alive, but did keep up a waiting list, so they never had to worry about filling a space.

Jon figured it would take them about three or four weeks to clean out the apartment, paint, clean the carpet, and replace the name on the brass plate. He doubted he'd still be around to see who that was. He planned to be back in New York with an acting job. But you never knew in his business. At least this so-called role was giving him some income and his agent could reach him easily enough. He'd be on a plane that same day if warranted.

Stepping from the apartment into the hallway, Jon was just in time to catch a glimpse of Harry Goldberg and Oscar Shapiro making their way towards the elevator with the petite Valeska Bernhart and her fancy dark mahogany cane with the silver handle between them. Her once famous legs were covered with a pair of black slacks, the fabric of which he couldn't make out. And she was wearing a fancy type of tennis shoe, not the three-inch spike heels she had always been photographed in.

As the trio shuffled towards the elevator, the newcomer to West Palm Acres told her companions that she was between thirty-one and death, had been married more times than she could remember, single now for thirteen or fifteen years. Warningly, in the event they had any ideas, she told them she didn't want to get married ever again. "Of course, I still have my mansion in Beverly Hills," she lied with a perfectly straight face, "in case this place doesn't work out for me. I never liked Florida. Too humid. Too blah. Servants are looking after the house. I didn't want to sub-let. They ruin the place. You know how that can be."

They didn't know how that can be, but completely in awe, shook their heads, mumbling in unison, "Ah."

Valeska had a captive audience and was milking it for all it was worth, adding or embellishing details, omitting certain others. Whatever made for a better story. Valeska Bernhart, the daughter of Minnie Rich and Herman Bernhart who came to the United States from Russia to start a new life in Brooklyn. Valeska Bernhart from Brooklyn to Hollywood to Beverly Hills to Santa Monica to West Palm Beach. It was at 2251 North Gower Street, Hollywood 28, California, where it almost didn't begin thanks to her eccentric neighbor, Pasha Elca (*nee* Elizabeth Cohen) from Brockton, Massachusetts, who claimed to be a scenario writer. Scenario writer? She couldn't write a note for the milkman. *Almost* didn't begin because the fool Pasha nearly burned down the place when she left her iron plugged in, and the next thing anyone knew, the fire department was there, saving the day, the apartment building, and a lot of lives. What else could be expected from a nut case like Pasha Elca who wrapped her money up in lettuce leaves in the ice-box? As if a burglar wouldn't look there first. Valeska moved to another place, still in Hollywood, and it wasn't long before she was noticed and began working in films; not just working, starring. Then came the husbands, the houses, the daughter, the downfall. It's a fact of life. What goes up eventually must come down. Rarely does it go back up again. Maybe if you're very very lucky or very very smart.

The gentlemen were riveted.

"When I splashed onto the screen, you know what they wrote in *Variety*? Quote: Valeska Bernhart is Technicolor even when she's in black and white. Unquote."

So absorbed in her story, the gentlemen forgot why they were standing at the elevator. It was Valeska who finally pressed the elevator 'down' button which only reinforced her theory that what goes up must come down.

2

VALESKA
A FEW YEARS EARLIER

She studied the reflection in the full-length mirror in her bedroom. Today, she would be facing her biggest challenge ever. It was the day she was going to an open casting call for an independent film to be produced and directed by an unknown twenty-two year old. Open casting calls were like meat markets. Every wannabe and his or her sister showed up. She was Valeska Bernhart. She had never had to go after a part. Producers and directors came to her. Scripts were delivered to her house for her to read in comfort while she lounged by the pool with champagne. Red grape juice had become the beverage of choice now. She convinced herself it was for health reasons rather than for economic reasons. Slightly easier to accept.

Until now, she couldn't bring herself to audition along with hundreds of others at an open call, but when the wolf is at the door, pride goes out the window. Having outlived three agents and two managers who had always kept her informed about the business, now she had to rely on weekly trade papers, but they were often out of date. What they listed as going on currently seemed to have already happened two weeks prior. Current happenings were on the Internet these days. If someone sneezed, it was out there before you could bless them. Being totally techno-phobic, but out of necessity, she had invested in a refurbished computer so she could at least get basic information. That's how she found out about Tara Bombeck's low budget film titled, *Murder in Key West*, briefly described as Harvard Business School professor in Key West for the Spring Break swims naked in the ocean at midnight, meets a shark, ends up in the hospital, falls in love with her male nurse, and if she lives, plans to marry him. First, they have to eliminate his pregnant wife. It was a flimsy story, but that was the least of Valeska's concerns. She rolled her eyes upward in disbelief and shrugged. With today's audience and their soap opera mentality, it just might work.

One last check in the mirror. Maybe not quite as statuesque as she once was, she still had one thing going for her—a gorgeous pair of gams. And she could still wear high heels to show them off. Never sure what to wear in early June, she had settled for the conservative two piece light blue silk suit, not new, but still stylish. In her opinion, good clothes never went out of fashion. With squinted eyes, she closed in on her face. Without the aid of plastic surgery, an apt description of the whole package might be a simple well-preserved. Anywhere else, that is, but not in Tinsel Town. In Hollywood, Valeska Bernhart had become invisible. There was a time just her first name filled the seats of cinemas and theatres. She made money, mostly for other people, but she hadn't done badly. All past tense.

Now she was facing the unpaid electricity bill and the overdue grocery bill. Her kind grocer, who remembered her from the old days, let it slide each month. And after eight years in one place, looming over her was the threat of eviction. The rent hadn't been paid for the past three months. Having become accustomed to the cozy apartment in the six-unit building in Santa Monica, she didn't want to move.

Cozy meant compact. Compact meant tiny. Tiny meant if your next door neighbor coughed, you got a sore throat. It wasn't like the good old days in her thirteen-roomed house in Bel Air; but neither was she living in one room over a stranger's garage in Bakersfield, God forbid.

Valeska locked her front door, went out to the small private parking area behind the building, and opened the door of her Plymouth. She climbed into her old relic with a faulty starter and wanted to vomit. How she longed for the days when she had beautiful cars and drivers, but she knew all too well what she had now was better than waiting at a bus stop, God forbid.

Not wanting to be late, she drove faster than she normally did. Not that it would matter if she were late. With an open casting call, there were no scheduled set appointments. She reminded herself she was still here, just down on her luck. It happened to everyone in show business at one time or another. Sly Stallone had only a hundred bucks in the bank, wrote *Rocky*, absolutely insisted he play the lead, and look what happened to him. It was a crazy business. Only people in the business knew how crazy.

Take the one she would be meeting today. This filmmaker, Tara Bombeck. Just out of film school and directing and producing her own film. An Indie. Studios were dead. It was all about the independent filmmakers. The business today was about youth. It would be Valeska's most challenging role to date, convincing the novice that this eighty—er, seventy-something actress could play a thirty year old character. She had been a star. Surely, Tara Bombeck could write her in somewhere. It didn't have to be the lead. Valeska had been taught to always think positive about any career move. To see the end before the beginning. Today, she saw herself coming away with a contract. Today, she would get a job. And her earnings would pay a few outstanding bills and be enough to buy her some time. More than that, it could mean a complete comeback.

Valeska found a space in the nearly full parking lot of what appeared to be an old warehouse. From what she could see, her car wasn't the only wreck. Somehow, this was not reassuring. She pulled down the visor and checked her face in the small mirror. First, the eyes. That's what people would see first. Her eyes were light violet and sparkled. The eyes don't change. The glue from the false lashes on her eyelids was beginning to itch, but she could live with it. She never even went to her mailbox without her eyelashes on. She checked other parts of her face. Rosy lipstick and cheeks were still fresh. Her skin was hydrated and would stay that way for another five hours before every crack and wrinkle reappeared, the cruel reminder the old gray mare ain't what she used to be. The thing on her head was made from human hair and looked real. Maybe a little too black. But still chic. Should she have gone for the light brown one today? Well, too late now. She flipped the visor back to its original place, took three slow, deep breaths, and exited the vehicle. She headed towards the entrance, swishing her hips and clicking her heels on the concrete, making full use of the trademark walk she invented years ago for one of her movie roles. In Hollywood, you never knew if the paparazzi were out and about. She took another deep breath and smiled, the old adrenaline rush kicking in for the first time in a long time.

The reception area was crowded, just as she knew it would be, each person hoping to fulfill a dream to get into the movies. Valeska paused briefly in the doorway, somewhat deflated that no one recognized her. She announced herself to the receptionist, was asked to add her name to a long list, and she asked for a script, only to be told there was no script to read, no scene to prepare. Times had certainly changed. She was handed a sheet of paper with the character breakdown list and a brief synopsis of the story. She started to explain that she already had this information, and then thought better about trying to talk to the male, or possibly female, gum-chewing person who was in charge.

Refusing to be disheartened, determined she wasn't going home without a job, Valeska found a seat among the sea of denim, and was sure she gave off an air of confidence and cheeriness, even if her insides were crumbling. The buzz around town and even in this room among the toddlers was about the fire on a back lot at Universal Studios earlier that week. Much was destroyed including nearly fifty thousand videos and reels, but fortunately, there were some duplicates in a different location. Two mock New York and New England streets used for movie making and tourist displays were a total loss. The cause of the fire was under investigation. Valeska had fond memories of filming at the studios and couldn't help taking it as a personal loss.

After nearly an hour of young things marching into the adjoining room to see the director–and marching out again with long faces, the receptionist called out her name, doing a hatchet job on the pronunciation. "Miss Barnhurd, you can go in now." He/she pointed to a door.

'Miss Barnhurd' let it go with a polite nod. As she always said, you can't kill a sparrow with a machine gun. Valeska took a deep breath and concentrated on her entrance into the unknown.

A large table, sufficing as the desk, and two metal chairs on opposite sides of the table/desk were the only pieces of furniture. Any minute, she expected a bat to fly down from the rafters. Obviously, it was all the production could afford. Surely, no one would choose this venue for auditions if one wasn't strapped for dough. The chairs didn't look very stable. Valeska hesitated before sitting down.

The seated Tara Bombeck looked up from the sheet of paper she was perusing and after a split second, her jaw literally fell open. Valeska's instincts were sharp. She waited, utterly relishing the moment that brought to mind a Buster Keaton silent film, Tara playing the Buster role, of course.

It was a few more seconds before Tara Bombeck could find her voice. It was the age of the actress standing before her that startled her at first. Hadn't she read the character breakdown? Then came recognition. She stood and, out of reverence, lowered her head and did a half-bow. "Good god, you're—"

"Not dead." Valeska jumped in with superb timing.

Not quite getting it, Tara said without a trace of humor, "No. No. I was going to say, Valeska Bernhart. You're Valeska Bernhart."

"Yes, I know," Valeska smiled.

"You're ancient." Quickly recovering, Tara added, "No, that's not what I meant to say."

"Forgotten. Well, here I am," Valeska cooed, quite thrilled at being recognized. So far, so good. It had begun on a high note. A very good sign.

Tara gushed on, "There was a marathon of yesteryear stars on Turner classics. A bunch of you. I saw it. You were great."

"Pity I missed that," Valeska said, feigning disappointment. She didn't think there was a need to mention that her cable had been cut off.

Letting Tara enjoy the moment of being in the presence of greatness, Valeska did a quick perusal of the short cropped copper haired Tara Bombeck. Every visible orifice was pierced with a silver loop stuck in it. Her knuckles were tattooed. The leather jacket was so worn, it looked like it was inside out. Her black jeans must have been painted on her body. Valeska wondered if she changed her thinning ash blonde—okay, white—hair color to an orange shade and got a crew cut and wore jeans, would she look younger? Maybe give up the black wig. She'd give it some thought. But not today. Today, she had other things on her mind.

"Here you have the legendary, thought to be retired or expired, Valeska Bernhart, seventy-sev…er…fifty-seven, give or take, insisting she can play a forty year old. Now isn't that a kick in the pants?" Valeska took the bull by the horns. No point pussy footing around. She had kept her voice light to sound like a young woman. If this was radio, listeners would have taken her for a teenager. With one eye on Tara, she sat down carefully on the unreliable looking chair, glad to get off her feet. She slowly and deliberately crossed her legendary legs at the knees.

Recovered from her earlier state of shock and adulation, Tara sat back in her chair and got down to business, stating in all seriousness, "The lead character is thirty-two. All the characters are in their twenties and thirties. I mean, Jesus, why are you here?"

Valeska ignored the nasty tone. "Really? Are you sure? She seemed so much more mature from the character description." Now they were equal, facing one another across the table. Valeska felt she might have a chance. Valeska knew a little bit about body language. Tara would have remained standing if there wasn't any hope.

"Didn't you read the character breakdown? Who's your agent for chrissakes?" Awe had turned to just plain annoyance. She was both aggravated and relieved at the interruption by her vibrating cell phone. Without so much as an 'excuse me, I have to take this,' she took the call. "What is it, Robbie? I'm in the middle of a meeting." Then Tara listened.

Valeska relaxed. A meeting. The director had said she was in a meeting. A very good sign. Very professional. She wasn't being tossed aside. Attention was being paid to Valeska Bernhart. She was in a meeting. She was being met.

And then Tara went berserk into the phone. "Are you shitting me? We shoot in four days. Every wannabe is sitting in the other room with their résumé of high school credits and a snapshot of their Community College graduation. Finding a fresh new face in Hollywood is like…like…I don't know what it's like. They all look alike. And now you've got the nerve to tell me you're bailing out to do a blockbuster? I brought you in as a favor, you little shit. You're no Max Factor. You're…" She stopped talking. "Hello? Hello? Don't you hang up on me!" She slammed the phone down on the table. "Friggin' pansy."

Valeska had taken in every word, picking up the gist. Tara was in trouble. It gave her an idea. This would be a good time to begin the schmooze. "I see your film as a kind of *Jaws* meets *General Hospital*." She moved her hand across the space in front of her face to indicate a screen. "Brilliant concept. In this business, if one waits long enough, something comes along that is so right. That's how I feel about this for me. I told that to Michael Caine just before he accepted the role in *Cider House Rules*." She was in. She could taste it. "Is this the script?" Valeska grabbed the manuscript from the table and clutched it to her chest as if it were the most precious object in the world. Right now, it was.

Tara's attempt to retrieve the script failed. "Listen, Miss Bernhart, I've seen two hundred actors in three days, and I still haven't found my lead. Really, there's nothing here for you."

"My dear, from what I understand, for most of the script, the heroine will be underwater or bandaged up in a hospital bed. Do you know how many films I've starred in? Do you know I played on Broadway?" Her earlier syrupy tone had turned sour and once out there, it couldn't be taken back.

"Like it isn't a question of whether or not you can act. Like there will be close-ups and nude scenes. The role is written for a much younger actress. Much."

Picking up the speech pattern of her nemesis, Valeska said, "Like put Vaseline on the lens."

"They do it with a nylon stocking now."

"Same result." Valeska batted her eyelids.

"There isn't anything for you," Tara stated firmly and stood up.

Like a child who ignores the parent's scolding, Valeska continued, "I could be the end of your search. Tell you what. I'll play myself. A cameo. Problem solved." She watched Tara closely for any telltale signs of life.

Tara protested, "Problem not solved. The script is frozen. No new characters. I need actors in their twenties and thirties. And I'm looking for an unknown to play the lead. I know it's crazy, but we think it will be great publicity."

"*American Idol* meets *America's Least Talented*," Valeska tossed out.

Tara looked at her blankly.

Valeska offered to read. She flipped through the pages looking for a scene, pretending she could see the type. Who was she kidding? She couldn't read a damned thing, and she wasn't going to fish in her handbag for her magnifying glass; the magnifying glass having been chosen over reading glasses strictly for economy rather than vanity in this particular case.

"There is nothing for you to read." Once again, Tara tried but failed to retrieve the script.

Valeska continued her sales pitch. "Did you know I played a thirty-two year old on Broadway when I was fifty-seven? I meant forty-five. Tennessee was astounded. Tennessee Williams. He wrote the part for me."

Despite feeling worn out, there was a part of Tara that

was fascinated. After all, this was Hollywood, and this woman was a living legend. And she had *chutzpah*, which in this business was the key to the kingdom. She suddenly remembered a lecture at UCLA. It was this very topic. Film versus Stage. "Maybe you can fool them on stage, but not on film. On film, your face is in their face. Every pore is a crevice."

Valeska couldn't let this *faux pas* pass without correction. "Quite the contrary, young lady. The stage is reality. You can't lie. Every breath must be the truth. You know what it feels like out there on stage every night and two matinees? It's like being eaten alive. Only the brave survive. With film, if you make a mistake, you can stop. In front of a live audience, that's not an option. You have to keep going. You have to get out of your own mistake. Believe me, kiddo, that's the test of a true actor. With film, the camera does the work. And now, heaven help us, computers have changed everything. If they can put a gorilla on the Empire State Building, think what you could do with my minor flaws." Valeska threw back her head and turned her face upwards to the left, displaying her better profile. "It's a director's medium, darling. Use your head. You could win an Oscar."

"You don't want me. You want Houdini, Tara snapped."

Valeska ignored the crack. Standing slowly, she was preparing to paint the picture. To sell the sizzle, as it were. The pitch.

When Valeska stood, Tara sat, somewhat defeated.

Valeska took center stage. "Think of it. We can bill it as my great comeback. You, an unknown, will become a household name. Of course, with the triumph, the men and in your case maybe the women will swarm around you. They will develop a crush on your talent. It's easy to believe the adoration is real. That's how I ended up with three, maybe four—I don't remember how many–lousy husbands, one who claimed to be a Count. He drained me dry, bank account-wise. You go dancing with that type, you don't marry them." It had been a while since she emoted with such gusto. It made her dizzy. She sat down.

As fascinating as the performance was, Tara wasn't buying. She reached across the table and once again tried to take the script out of Valeska's hands. "There's nothing for you here. I'm sorry. I have a lot of people to see. I really have to move on. On top of everything, my make-up guy just bailed."

Advantage Valeska. The scoreboard had changed. She sensed a kind of desperation in Tara's voice. Time to move in with her back-up plan devised during the previous phone call. "Miss Bombeck, I just had an idea." Valeska brought her voice right up to her top register to sound innocent the way Bette Davis often did in her movies. "I could be the end of your search."

"Been there, dear. Sorry. Thank you for coming in." Tara stood and nodded towards the door. "Go."

Eyes straight ahead, steady as a boulder, Valeska held her position.

"We're done here, Miss Bernhart."

What was next? Physical force? Valeska didn't move.

Tara called out towards the door, "Security!"

"Save your breath. It's just you and me, Miss Bombeck."

"Okay, okay, I understand. You want to work. Have you thought of doing commercials?"

"Commercials!" That's when Valeska blew her cool. "What? Dentures? Depends? Cat food? I hate cats. And I wear neither Depends nor dentures. All my own, baby!" She opened her mouth wide and flashed a mouthful of teeth and gums in Tara's face.

"Yes, yes, they're lovely. You'll have to give me the name of your dentist. Look, it isn't a stigma anymore to do commercials. They've all done it. Lauren Bacall, June Allyson, even Bobby DeNiro, I think. Look, there really isn't anything for you in this one. Like, I'm really sorry." And she was. Almost.

Valeska would have to switch tactics. It was time to soften the tough Gloria Swanson/*Sunset Boulevard* act. It wasn't working. Next, she did humble and hated herself with every word she uttered. "A surgeon in the hospital. A few lines. Let people know I'm still here." She was doing something she had never had to do. Beg. Maybe about the rent; about the groceries; but not when it came to her art. "Of course, everyone knows comedy is my forte, but I'm sure you'd allow me to put my own slant on the role; you know, lighten it up."

Tara was not about to give a charitable donation. "You have to leave. I can't believe your agent sent you."

"Darling, I've outlived three agents and two managers," Valeska said flatly.

Tara had to sit down again. She knew it was giving a message of hope to this woman seated across from her, but she was exhausted and the consignment shop two sizes too small like new alligator boots were positively murdering her.

Valeska was hoping that somewhere under Tara's mottled leather jacket, there was a beating heart. "Miss Bombeck, I...I haven't worked in...in quite a while. I don't have any other talent. I'm an artist. There are bills to pay. Maybe you know how that can be. I'll do anything as long as I get paid for it. Anything." She meant it, but she didn't know how much she meant it until she heard it out loud. The voice came from deep inside her. She slowly released the script she had been clutching to her bosom and placed it back on the table. "It isn't a good thing to want to work and not be able to. An artist without art might as well be dead. I don't want to have to move. I live in Santa Monica. I like it." She had said it. She had said her humiliation out loud. How humiliating was that!

Tara twitched. Something surfaced that she had stuffed away. Her mother was on the horizon as a costume designer in films when her father walked out on them. She took the split up hard and started drinking. Her mother's career soured, and she had to take employment as a seamstress in a dress shop to support them. It was a far cry from the lights of a sound stage. Suddenly concerned about this human being in front of her, Tara asked, "What about family? Didn't I read somewhere you had a daughter?"

Valeska nearly knocked the chair over when she stood. "Ha! My advice? Don't have children. My daughter married a nothing. They bought a sushi restaurant near Miami Beach. She grew up surrounded by servants. She spoke fluent French when she was eight. She could have been a great pianist. Instead, she's making a way of life out of seaweed and rice."

"Sushi is very popular. Everyone eats sushi now."

"Raw fish in all that heat? My god!" Valeska hollered. "When I wanted Japanese food, my manager made arrangements for me to tour Tokyo. That's stardom, kiddo." The pitch was being resurrected. It wasn't over yet. "We wore chiffon and lace, and the diamonds weren't on loan like they do now. I kept mine in a safe. They sent Rolls-Royces and Bentleys, not these ugly stretch limousines today that they think are glamorous." Valeska had Tara's full attention. She knew when to move and when to pause, when to look at her audience, when to look away, when to raise the tone of her voice, and when to lower the tone. She leaned ever so slightly into Tara across the table. "You know what my daughter has on her wall in the restaurant?" Not waiting for Tara's reply, she sailed on, quite proud of the event that inspired the tale she was about to unfold.

"A telegram from Noel Coward. You do know who Noel Coward is, don't you? December 16, 1960." She recited the exact date with great pride. "A small catered gathering at my house in honor of Noel's and my mutual birthdays. Not the same year, of course. All of a sudden, my daughter brought out a surprise from the kitchen. Surprise? I was flabbergasted. She had cooked a pot roast. She was just a kid. I don't know how she knew how to do that. We used to hire people to change light bulbs, never mind to do the cooking. Anyway, she served it to Noel. Being a gentleman, he ate a decent amount. The next day, a telegram arrived for my daughter. 'Darling, Anna. The pot roast was a hit. Love, Noel Coward.' That telegram is hanging on the wall of that sushi restaurant near Miami Beach. Imagine that. On the wall."

Tara knew her schedule had gone haywire, that she had lost control, but as a budding filmmaker, she couldn't dismiss this private moment with a living legend who was neurotic but totally mesmerizing. The real source of Valeska's ache had surfaced. "Like, I'm going to jump in here; maybe stick my neck out. When was the last time you saw your daughter?"

Valeska felt faint and sat down. "I don't know. When they opened the restaurant. 1997, I think. Maybe '98. I can't remember. My granddaughter was just a baby. Now she's getting married in five weeks. I don't know anything about the boy. I don't know what kind of a family he comes from. I know nothing. You know how I heard of it? I got an invitation in the mail. Like a stranger. Not even a phone call."

There it was. The desperation. Intentionally ignoring the obvious point here, Tara said, "That is so great. You have a wedding to go to. It's beyond great."

"Great? What's so great about it? You think I'm going? I have a set of silver fruit knives that belonged to my mother. They'll get those for a present, not my presence," Valeska spat out. Getting the invitation in the mail was a crushing blow. She was near to tears, but whatever she said or did here today, she would not let herself cry in front of this stranger.

"So you see how you can help. I would prefer not to lie to my family when I tell them I'm w-o-r-k-i-n-g," she said, spelling out the word. "That is where you come in, toots."

"Tara." Suddenly she had an idea. It was a long shot, but she, too, was desperate. Maybe it would work. She explained her problem about the make-up. Apart from not having a lead for the film, her make-up person got an offer to do a blockbuster and had bailed out. He'd been her last resort. Absolutely everyone she knew was unavailable. "Do you know anyone?" she asked, knowing full well what she was doing. It was her turn to pitch.

"They're all dead." But I'm not, Valeska thought. Planting the seed, she said nonchalantly, "I often did my own make-up. Unusual, I know, but I'm gifted."

"Really?" This might work. It would serve them both. "Many stars work both ends of the camera now. Bob Redford and Clint and Goldie and Joanne Woodward. Have you ever considered it? Great stuff on the bio."

"I don't care for directing. Not that I wouldn't be wonderful at it." Valeska knew what she was doing.

"Actually, that's my job," Tara said quickly. "I don't mean that. I'm talking about the costume designers, the camera men and women, art directors. So much goes into making a movie. It's a team effort. It isn't just about the actors." Tara studied her target. "What about the make-up artists? Stars in their own right."

Caught up in the image, Valeska recalled some of the wonderful make-up artists she had known. "Wally Westmore. William Tuttle. Ben Nye. What would have happened to dear Judy Anderson? A great stage actress, but she could never have made it on screen without Guy Pearce slapping the pancake on her." Valeska would take it to her grave that she was passed up for the role they gave to Judith Anderson in *Laura*. She justified the decision by telling herself that leading lady Gene Tierney didn't want any competition in the looks department.

"Valeska Bernhart, you have given me an idea."

"I have? What's that?" Valeska was good at playing dumb when she needed to.

"You have solved my problem. Well, one of my problems." She was good at playing dumb, too.

"Oh?"

"I'd like to offer you the job, no, not job, the *role* of Make-up Artist on *Murder in Key West*." Tara held her breath, not wanting to kill it with too many words in the first sentence. Then she continued with her sales pitch.

Valeska believed she had engineered it, but she'd have to pretend she wasn't interested. She didn't want to sound too anxious. She caught the end of Tara's spin.

"…can get three thousand actors to play one role, but if you can do make-up, we bow down to you."

Valeska knew the 'we' were the producers, directors, writers, so on and so forth. Wanting to play it cool, she didn't speak; just "ah-ha."

Tara had her now. Coaxing sweetly, but with an edge, she said, "Remember your little cozy cocoon in Santa Monica? You don't want to have to give that up."

"Home sweet home," Valeska said.

"Home sweet home," Tara repeated.

Valeska was being snowed, but it didn't cost anything to let Tara think it had all been her own idea. Valeska knew she had set the wheels in motion. That was enough for her. She hemmed and hawed for effect. "Gosh, gee, I don't know. It's a big shift."

The negotiations were on. "I can tell you're thinking about it. That's good."

Valeska was in the game. "Better than shifting into a room over someone's garage, God forbid. Ha. Ha."

Tara was tired of this cat and mouse game now. She needed to close. "So you'll do it?"

Valeska said very pointedly, "I can think of a million reasons why I shouldn't…and only one why I should."

"I take it that's a yes. Great. That is so great," Tara squealed. Jesus, Bombeck, get a grip.

"Of course, we'll be on location in Key West?" Valeska asked.

"Sorry, low budget. We're shooting the whole picture right here in Los Angeles. You can sleep in your own bed every night. Isn't that wonderful?" Tara made it sound like it was an Academy Award.

Valeska said she would need a script, a contract, and all that. Tara reassured her she would get it all as soon as she had a cast. Valeska explained she was between agents but was sure they could work it out. She knew enough about the money part to do the deal herself. "I don't come cheap." But as she said it, she knew she would work for minimum wage. Money was money. And maybe she could convince Tara *not* to list her name on the credits. Not convince; insist.

"Awesome. Of course, there are some legal issues we'll have to work out. You know, the union and all that, but it can be done." She had no intention of billing Valeska in the credits, but she'd deal with that later. "More actors should be independent like you. Welcome aboard, Valeska Bernhart." Tara stood and held out her right hand.

"I don't shake," Valeska said politely but firmly.

"Understood." Tara withdrew her hand.

"You'll be sending a car?" Valeska asked.

"Budget again, Valeska, sorry. Not even for the actors."

Valeska got it. It was the old story. Show business. When you can afford it, they give you everything. When you can't afford it, you have to pay. And then Valeska said something very profound, something she hoped one day to really believe. "I guess you don't have to love what you do as long as you love *why* you do it."

"Meaning?" Tara was perplexed.

"Miss Bombeck, come on. We both got something. Even if it wasn't exactly our first choice." Valeska made a mental note to be careful what she asked for in the future. All she prayed for that morning was a job. God wasn't that smart. In future, she would have to specify.

Tara stood and shouted in the direction of the reception area, "Next!"

Recognizing a cue, Valeska stood, too. "Your star is on the horizon, Tara Bombeck." Boy, was it a new horizon. The deal was done. No verbal representation of a goodbye, just a nod from both of them was all that was necessary.

Always mindful that in Hollywood hidden cameras could be anywhere, a now smiling Valeska Bernhart began her pointed departure using her trademark walk. With a dignified swagger, she exited the scene of what could only be labeled as 'the trade-off.'

3

THE ROAD TO WEST PALM BEACH

4-J West Palm Acres had become home for Valeska. After a month, she felt more settled and actually enjoyed not having to cook and do all that domestic stuff. It hadn't been an easy decision to finally leave Hollywood. Valeska realized she didn't have a choice. She could no longer sustain herself. The career was over. Her star didn't shine anymore. She was a has-been. A *has-been*. What a lousy way to describe retirement. Okay, forced retirement.

To face reality had been tough. To finally admit there weren't going to be enough film offers hit her hard. To finally admit she couldn't afford to live alone anymore had been a gut wrenching scene. And to finally admit she couldn't drive anymore hit her below the belt. And when she looked in the mirror, despite the 8-watt pink light bulbs she now plugged in her lamps, she was old. In the race with time, time had won. It comes to everyone and how she hated to be like everyone.

Her daughter came through when it mattered and said she would subsidize Valeska's social security, but only if she moved to Florida. Valeska surrendered and the search began to find accommodations. And since Anna was footing most of the bill, which wasn't cheap, Valeska was determined to make it work.

She could never understand her daughter's life choices with all the advantages she had had. Valeska always suspected the man she married was gay. It was all hushed up, but most everyone knew his *business* partner in the restaurant was really his *friend*. It was never discussed in the family. What was the difference? They were waiting for her to die so they could get their hands on the two diamond rings, the diamond bracelet, and the sapphire and diamond pin that had all belonged to her mother. Valeska had never actually shown the jewels to them. It was simply assumed they were in a safe deposit box at the bank. Fortunately none of Valeska's husbands knew about those pieces. They'd taken everything else. But that was history. As a matter of fact, so were the jewels. When the work dried up, she was forced to sell it all. She had lived on the proceeds of the sale for as long as she could. And then it was over.

She made that dreaded call to her daughter who helped with the move. There wasn't much to move. And here she was. After about a month, she began to feel more comfortable in her new home. She was meeting other residents and discovered she liked the activities and the social aspect. You could be alone if you wanted privacy or you just had to step outside your front door and there were people. She was settling in to West Palm Acres quite nicely. And even though her family lived an hour away, they didn't visit, which was okay to Valeska.

4

HOLLYWOOD EAST AND NEW YORK SOUTH

Four weeks ago, Jon Sullivan stood outside 4-H on his first day, expecting Hank Herman. As it turned out, Hank Herman had been the former occupant. It was a painfully huge reminder to Jon that he was still there. There hadn't been a nibble on an acting role, a commercial, or print work. Nothing. So he stayed on. The upside was he was missing a brutal winter up north.

He looked at his list on the clipboard and back up at the nameplate. **Glick Glickman.** Glick Glickman was not an unfamiliar name to Jon. He knew Glick Glickman, if indeed it was *the* Glick Glickman. Not *knew* knew. In the business, who didn't know him or of him? Jon once did an audition for an off-Broadway revival of *Waiting for Godot*. Glick was the director. Anyway, Jon didn't get the part. They exchanged a few words. Glick was very polite, said he'd keep Jon in mind for the future. Blah, blah, blah. All that kind of talk that no one means and no one believes. Still, at the time, it's nice to hear. Better than a kick in the back seat. But Jon didn't really think this was *the* Glick Glickman. At West Palm Acres? And yet, how many Glick Glickmans could there be? Just in case he was the genuine article, Jon decided to go for broke. He took a deep breath, puffed himself up and rapped lightly on the lime green door. Knock first, then the dialogue. Never at the same time lest the verbal message be muffled by the sound. He said a silent thank you to Acting 101.

With Royal Academy of Dramatic Art diction, he called out, "Mister Glick Glickman, it's time to take your pill!" *Mister Glick Glickman.* Why did he do that? He was only supposed to call out the last name. He felt like a dunce. Although, calling out the full name did give it an element of class.

While waiting for a response, he couldn't help wonder what kind of medication Glick Glickman was on; if indeed, it was *that* Glick Glickman. Jon had read about the catastrophic Broadway failure, the flop that never opened. After that, Glick couldn't get going with anything. Lots of directors were known to suffer severe coronaries due to the pressure of show business. Maybe he was on some kind of heart medicine; maybe some kind of sedative. But Jon wasn't allowed to ask or to be apprised of these matters. He shouldn't even be speculating on a matter that was none of his business. Not usually a nosy type of person, he felt embarrassed. He waited a few beats and knocked again, this time with a heavier hand using his closed fist.

He cleared his throat and called out into the door, "Mister Glickman, it's time to take your pill!" He put his ear against the door to see if he could hear any life inside.

After a few seconds, a gravelly voice mixed with a touch of honey bellowed, "Yeah, yeah, I heard ya the first time. Now you hear this. Beat it."

Jon knew for certain now. Either Glick Glickman had a twin brother or it was the man himself. That voice could only belong to one person. It was *that* Glick Glickman on the other side of the door. Jon would have loved to see the man face to face; maybe remind him they had met. On second thought, he knew it couldn't be under the present circumstances. Not with him, a serious actor, dressed in a clown suit reminding people to take their medicine. And he didn't know what frame of mind Glick Glickman was in. Maybe he was hiding out of shame. Maybe he wouldn't appreciate being reminded. Jon knew his place and moved on to 4-J.

The place was becoming a regular Hollywood East and New York South. First, Valeska Bernhart; and now, Glick Glickman. Jon's hand was in position ready to knock when the door opened. Who should appear in the doorway of Valeska Bernhart's apartment on their way out? None other than the odd couple, Harry Goldberg and Oscar Shapiro. Jon could just imagine the conversations between the two movie buffs and the former film star. Images from the *Road* pictures with Dorothy Lamour, Bob Hope, and Bing Crosby flooded his brain. *The Road to West Palm*. He was caught laughing out loud by Harry Goldberg.

"What's so funny? I took the pill a quarter of an hour ago," said Harry. He said it with complete conviction even though it wasn't his turn to be reminded.

Out of habit, Jon asked Oscar Shapiro if he had taken his pill. Oscar nodded. Jon wasn't sure if that meant he had taken it or he hadn't taken it. Jon couldn't let it go. He took his responsibilities seriously. Once again, he checked with Harry and Oscar. Once again, they said they had taken their medication. Jon couldn't take an x-ray of their stomachs, so he had to believe them. Anyway, theoretically, it wasn't their time since they were in someone else's apartment. Now that that was more or less sorted out, he took the opportunity to ask if they had met the recent arrival. Like some kind of spy on a secret mission, he tilted his head and rolled his eyes towards 4-H.

"Oh, him. Glickman. Met him in the elevator. We're good friends," Harry 'know-it-all' Goldberg said.

Jon didn't believe him. Judging from the response he just got when he knocked on the door, Glick probably would have taken the stairs to avoid people or never left his apartment.

"Don't listen to Harry. Glickman stays mostly in his apartment. Orders take-out or eats out a lot. He has a car," Oscar volunteered.

"She," Harry said, indicating Valeska's door with a nod of his head, "can't stand him."

"Really?" said Jon who was most curious. "They know each other?"

"Never met him; doesn't want to," offered Oscar. "I know this for a fact."

"I do, too," said Harry, not wanting to be outdone. "She told us."

He didn't believe that he and Valeska had never met. How would she know she couldn't stand him if they had never met? "So it really is Glick Glickman, the Broadway impresario?" Jon asked, wanting confirmation.

Oscar and Harry shook their heads up and down.

Oscar said, "He doesn't talk to anyone."

Harry added, "For hours, he sits on the verandah on one of those rockers out there without saying a word. Just stares out into nothing."

"For hours," Oscar said.

"I just said that," Harry corrected him.

Ignoring him, Oscar said, "Sometimes he sits on the bench in the garden. Just sits. I can see him from the dining room."

"Isn't he a little too young to be here?" asked Jon.

"Are you kidding?" said Harry Goldberg. "He's been under the knife so many times his face is in the back of his head."

For some reason, that remark cracked up Oscar Shapiro. He practically doubled over with laughter.

Never able to resist a one-liner, Harry Goldberg said, "Careful you shouldn't hurt yourself."

Jon couldn't help wonder what really made brash, fast-talking, quick-witted Glick Glickman the withdrawn person he had now become.

A LITTLE REVUE BY GLICK GLICKMAN
A COUPLE OF YEARS EARLIER

Characters in order of appearance

Jane Smith, an assistant
Rocky Rage, an actor
Inky Krabb, an actress
Ruby Valk, an actress
Enzo Bordello, an actor

With purpose, Jane Smith entered the bright rehearsal studio in mid-Manhattan. She carried her belongings and tools of the trade: a large canvas bag containing the manuscript, a legal pad, several pencils with erasers, and some personal items. Her hair was attempting to be a pony tail, not quite making it. The heavy black framed eyeglasses were too large for her narrow face. Her attire was what might be called practical, rather than stylish; yet, there was something appealing about the twenty-eight year old, depending on who was looking. At the moment, no one was looking.

Lounging on a threadbare prop couch in the center of the room was twenty-something beefy framed actor, Rocky Rage. He was reading the funnies in a newspaper and, as usual, eating. This time, a Hershey Bar with Almonds whose wrapper he had casually dropped on the floor.

Annoyed, and in a mildly authoritative manner, Jane said, "Please don't eat the props, Mr. Rage."

Rocky looked up at Jane. Ignoring the reference to the props, he said indifferently, "Good morning, Jane. I like your hair. It's…" he struggled for the right word… "uncomplicated."

Without taking offense, Jane replied, "My fuses blew." She fingered some of the strands of the damp hair.

Rocky got back to his literature, periodically taking bites out of his candy bar.

Jane went about her business getting the rehearsal studio ready for rehearsal. That was part of her job as general assistant, stage manager, gofer to Glick Glickman, theatrical producer, director, playwright, and so many other things. He was the man with whom Jane was secretly in love. She wanted to shout it from the rooftops, but a secret is a secret.

Funny lady, Inky Krabb, twenty-three according to her résumé, breezed in, her usual jovial manner evident, with a tote bag containing her script and personal items slung over a shoulder. "Morning everybody," she sang. When she didn't get any response, she went on, "Ah, everybody isn't here." Not that she cared. Rocky was there, and that's all that mattered to her. She greeted Jane with a salute and said, "I like your hair."

"My fuses blew."

Solely for Rocky's benefit, Inky declared, "I love mornings, don't you? I think it's something to do with waking up." Still getting no reaction from the actor she secretly loved, she continued, "I love nuts and raisins, too. Doesn't mean I eat fruitcake." Still no reaction. When a skinny comic gets no reaction from a fat comic, she has no choice but to carry on. "I like fresh strawberries. Doesn't mean I like strawberry ice-cream." As if afflicted with some kind of verbal ailment, she went on, "Howdy doo, Rocky Rage. So, ya wanna be on the stage. There's one leaving in twenty minutes. Ha. Ha." Determined to get Rocky's attention, there was no stopping her now. "Gimme an R, gimme an O, gimme a C, gimme a K, gimme a Y. Yeah, Rocky!" Her mouth was on automatic pilot. "I woke up this morning, checked it off my list, threw a four leaf clover over my shoulder, and here I am. What's your story?" Still no response. Totally deflated, she eyed her competition. "How's your Hershey Bar?"

Rocky ignored her babblings and grabbed a mini-bag of potato chips from the prop table. It meant he had to elevate himself from the couch which he did with a groan, but he quickly returned to his horizontal position; thus, feeling happy again. Ripping open the bag, he said nonchalantly, "When I was a kid, we had a dog that could rip open a bag of potato chips."

"You had a dog that ate potato chips?" Inky was delighted with what she happily interpreted as the opening of a dialogue with her dream man.

"Naw," Rocky replied. "He got bored after he opened the bag. He walked away, and I ate them. I ate the bag, too." Rocky quickly devoured the contents and let the empty bag slip to the floor.

Jane jumped to action and rushed over to pick it up along with the candy wrapper with a kind of "tsk" sound, placing the items in a make-shift receptacle; actually, just a cardboard box.

"Whoa, you ate the bag?" Inky asked in disbelief, but thrilled at the prospect of a discussion.

"So my mother wouldn't know," he replied casually.

"I did that with lollipops." Here was a common ground. She was on her way to a union.

Jane was in earshot and said, "Lollipops don't come in a bag."

"Excuse me, but this is a private conversation." Inky had Rocky's full attention now, and there was no way it was going to become a *ménage a trois*.

Jane knew when she wasn't wanted and exited to another room that wasn't really a room, just sort of an entrance hall cum foyer.

"So about the lollipops," Inky went on, wanting to keep Rocky's attention as long as possible. "I first discovered lollipops when I was five. I wasn't supposed to eat them because my mother said that dentists cost money. So I hid the sticks under my bed. She worked with my father in his delicatessen and never cleaned the house. Then we moved. That's when she found out. There were about a million sticks under my bed."

"My cousin Stanley swallowed a lollipop whole once," Rocky remembered.

"That's terrible. What happened?" Inky asked.

"He became a psychiatrist and worked it out."

Inky wasn't sure if he was joking or telling the truth. In case it was a joke, she made sounds to express amusement.

Rocky became more interested in the mint he found in between the old cushions on the sofa than in lollipops.

Inky got the message. End of *that* discussion. "Well, where is everybody? You'd think they'd be so happy to be working again that they'd be here on time." She sat down on one of the four stools placed stage left. "I'm gonna complain to Glickman." As she said it, she knew complaining wasn't possible. She couldn't complain to the producer about the director because the producer was the director and also the playwright.

"Let's face it. Without him, we haven't got a thing," Rocky said earnestly.

"We got us. He may have thought up the idea, but without us, those characters are just black letters on a page without a breath between them. We give them life."

Rocky didn't agree. "Aw, come on. The truth is for the past three years, I've been slinging hash in a cheap diner."

Inky hated when he put himself down and reminded him he had done TV commercials.

Rocky wasn't uplifted. "Two in three years didn't exactly make me rich. Aspirin and acne cream. Big deal. What about you?"

"A singing waitress in an Italian restaurant and a floor manager at Wal-Mart." It had been a dark period for Inky Krabb. But she did take solace in the fact she had worked her way up from cashier. "Youngest employee ever at a Wal-Mart," she said with some pride. No, wait, not pride; anguish.

"I'd leave that one off your professional résumé." He felt hopeful about their current project. Glick Glickman had pulled off some great deals in the past and it was hoped he could do it again. "The point is if Glick Glickman can get this show off the ground, and it looks like we're there, we're back in business. The business will be back in business."

Inky had been on her way. They all were. But that was before. Then it was over. Broadway simply went out of business. Theatres closed. There wasn't any money. Audiences couldn't pay the exorbitant ticket prices. Over a hundred dollars for a decent seat. Legitimate theater was in crisis mode. Until now. Maybe. If they were a smash hit. It was a big 'if.'

Jane came back in, resetting fresh, edible props. She hovered listening to their conversation. She didn't want to miss anything about Glick Glickman.

Rocky said, "Personally, I kiss the ground that Glick Glickman walks on."

Despite her bravado, Inky had her doubts. "You really believe *A Little Revue* is gonna make it? If you ask me, it's a stupid title."

Rocky reassured her they were terrific and could make it happen. "Our little company, when the other two decide to get here, can do it. We four in this vehicle are the great hope for the return of Broadway, not just for us, but for every actor who ever walked the boards. For everyone in love with the theatre. By the way, I think it's a great title. It's clever. It says what it is."

Despite Rocky's reassurances, Inky was worried. For the past two weeks, they had sat around talking about it. No one had seen the second act. She doubted it was even written. They were to open in a week. And where was their director/playwright? Rocky said he was probably working on the ending and suggested that instead of yapping about it, they should just do their sketch in the first act. Inky was being obstinate. She needed their director to rehearse. Rocky insisted.

"With her standing around watching us?" Inky said, glancing at Jane.

Jane was highly insulted. She was the assistant. She was supposed to stand around and watch. Inky and Rocky got out their scripts, each one insisting they knew it, but still liked holding the script, in case. They began, in character.

ROCKY: Okay, lady, put 'em up. This ain't no water pistol.

Jane rushed over and handed Rocky a prop gun. He took it without coming out of character.

ROCKY: Your American Express card or I'll shoot.

INKY: So shoot.

Rocky jabbed the gun in her back. Inky, out of character, said, "Ouch. That hurts." Rocky told her to stay in character.

ROCKY: Quit stallin'.

INKY: I'll give you anything. Take my Pierre Cardin gold and emerald bangle. Take my Cartier's diamond ring. Take my mink-lined trench coat. Take anything. Anything. Take me!

Inky threw her arms around Rocky and pressed into him—it was the part she liked best. Slowly they sank to the floor.

INKY: But don't take my American Express card.

ROCKY: American Express gives you more than just a card.

At this precise moment, the third member of the cast, who was the love of Rocky's life, made her entrance. Coming out of character, he extricated himself from Inky's grip and stood up leaving his scene partner huddled up on the cement floor.

Dark-haired leading lady, glamorous thirty year old, Ruby Valk swept in. She did not return Rocky's affections, but harbored feelings for their handsome leading man, Enzo Bordello who hadn't arrived yet. She had hoped to arrive last, making a spectacular grand entrance solely for Enzo. When she became aware he wasn't there, she dropped the pose.

Jane rushed over and said with much aplomb, "You look stunning as always, Miss Valk." She half curtsied and took Ruby's black mohair, pretending to be cashmere, cape and placed it on the prop table.

"Oh, hang it, dear, hang it," Ruby instructed firmly, rolling her eyes to the ceiling.

To Jane, Ruby was royalty. She picked up the wrap, unsure where to hang it. They went through this ritual every morning. It always ended up draped over the arm of the couch. Rocky always hoped no one saw him sniffing it.

Ruby studied Jane. "Your hair, dear. It's...uncomplicated."

"My fuses blew," said Jane, rather thrilled that Ruby had noticed.

Rocky was secretly in love with Ruby Valk and as remote a dream as it was, he longed for the nights when she would be spending them with him. But he knew in his heart a fat comic had more of a chance of winning the lottery than the heart of Ruby Valk. Still...the dream provided him with a colorful fantasy life. "Good morning, Ruby. Did you have a nice evening?" It didn't come out as sincerely as he had hoped.

Dismissing him like he was a lowly bug, Ruby said, "A dedicated actress spends her evenings at home with her script."

Still on the floor where Rocky had left her, Inky said, "I understand for the past several years you spent your evenings somewhere else."

Ruby glared at her, a mere speck. "We all had to earn a living, Miss Krabb."

"Let's get this show on the road. I came to rehearse. I expect to rehearse." Inky despised the fact that the object of her affections had his sights on another. "Come on, we've waited long enough. It's show time. I could use a good laugh."

Jane took umbrage and let them have it. "It isn't a show. It's a revue in words and movement based on a play based on an original short story by Glick Glickman."

Ruby muttered, "I feel like I'm in the twilight zone."

Rocky came to her defense. "You haven't a thing to worry about. You're Ruby Valk."

"Thank you, Rocky. You're a dear. You couldn't hurt a fly," Ruby said without any conviction.

Ever the comic and ever jealous of Rocky's obvious affection for Miss Valk, Inky said out of the side of her mouth, "Did ya hear `bout the gal who was afraid of flies until she opened one?"

"I don't understand. Was she a biologist?"

"Oh, the pain of it." Inky was indeed in agony. Ruby's retort cut below the belt.

"Pain is what drives me on. Pain is what makes me great." Ruby had taken center stage, not that she'd been off it.

"Why do you make such a drama of everything?" Inky was fed up with her.

"In case you hadn't a clue, Miss Krabb, drama is my business," Ruby spat out. It was an oldie but a goodie and she used the retort often.

Rocky couldn't stand to see Ruby upset. To diffuse the situation, he turned the conversation to himself. "If I can make people laugh, then I'm happy. I'll have plenty of opportunity in this production. It's a funny script."

Ruby didn't agree. She thought the script was just so-so. "We are what will make it funny. We have to. The entire world is watching." Head high, she added haughtily, "That's the royal we."

Rocky wanted to tell her how wonderful she was and that she could never let anyone down, but his shyness in the presence of astonishing greatness wouldn't allow it.

Inky, on the other hand, wanted to throw up. Feeling most insecure, she fished around in her bag for her mirror. Finding it, she glanced at her face. "Something's wrong with this mirror. I look terrible."

Jane was concerned. "Aren't you feeling well, Miss Krabb?"

"How should I know how I feel? I'm an actress. A figment of someone else's mind. Do I exist at all?" Inky's answer had the makings of a dragged out monologue until she was interrupted by the sound of loud tapping coming from the outer hall and getting closer.

Enzo Bordello, the fourth member of the company, made his grand entrance with a walking stick. This prop was a new addition to his appearance. The handsome leading man who claimed to be thirty-seven give or take a few years mostly give, carried a Louis Vuitton leather bag that had seen better days, but as the saying goes, 'buy good and it will last.' His entrance was made even grander by his recitation. "Once upon a midnight dreary, while I pondered weak and weary, over many a quaint and curious volume of forgotten love, so forth and so on. Suddenly there came a tapping, rapping at my chamber door, blah, blah, blah. Only this and nothing more." With perfect timing, Enzo paused, lowered his head for effect, got none, looked up, and smiled. His bleached teeth literally could have blinded anyone who was looking in that direction. And they all were looking.

There was much applause from Ruby, Inky, Rocky, Jane, and especially from Enzo who loved putting his hands together for himself. While Inky was in love with Rocky and Rocky was in love with Ruby and Ruby was in love with Enzo and Jane was in love with Glick and Glick was in love with the deal, Enzo was in love with Peter O'Toole whom he'd never actually met.

"I'd love to do Shakespeare one day," Rocky said to Ruby hoping to impress her.

"It was Edgar Allen Poe, idiot," she said, wanting to impress Enzo. The smoothness and richness of Enzo's voice sent a tingling sensation down her spine like hot chocolate fudge melting on ice cold vanilla ice-cream on a summer's day.

Rocky's bubble burst when Ruby corrected him.

Hoping to win points with Enzo, Ruby added, "Beautiful, Enzo, just beautiful."

"Poe, shmoe." Inky didn't understand a word.

Enzo acknowledged Ruby's praise with a nod and embraced the troupe with his eyes. "Is everyone splendid?" He caught sight of Jane's hair. "Ah, Jane. Dear, sweet Jane. So… uncomplicated."

In unison, Rocky, Inky, and Ruby cried out, "Her fuses blew."

Not ready to give up center stage, Enzo reviewed the history that had brought him to this point. "I was in my last production on Broadway four years ago this very month. Of course, I didn't know it at the time. Little did any of us dream our closing night party really was closing night for nearly the entire business. Plays got too big and prices too high. In order to justify this and give the audience a big bang for their buck, casts grew. But when the players outnumber the theatre patrons in the house...well…" He shrugged and threw up his hands. "It was difficult for dedicated thespians to make the adjustment. Play reading groups grew up, but no new plays were being written. Some went to Los Angeles, the city of angels. Most took jobs outside the business just to pay the rent. If Glick Glickman pulls this off, it will be the renaissance of what is left of the Broadway theatre."

Inky was skeptical, despite her earlier confidence. "It's only a tiny production. Do you really think it's big enough?"

"It has us," Ruby said. "That counts for something."

Rocky agreed. "It's brilliant."

Inky was convinced it might just be a one shot deal and after it was over, she'd be demonstrating cheese dip in grocery stores. "Retail, here I come."

Ruby said it would never happen to her. She said she would take to the streets before that happened. On top of everything, she was very annoyed that Glick was an hour late. "I loathe shoddiness."

Enzo reassured her. "That was never Glick Glickman's style. He's very smart. He knows he's done his job. It's up to the four of us now. We will be the ones out on that stage, breathing as one. His absence has created a kind of mutiny in us. He has stepped aside when the time came. We've become a close knit unit. Don't you see? The four of us are one. The man's a genius."

Ruby was nervous. She needed the job. "Our lives are in the hands of a man who is a quasi-businessman without a creative bone in his body. Think about it." There was a moment while they each pondered the genius of Glick Glickman. Ruby went on, "When he is here, he's always on the phone. As an entrepreneur, he has other businesses going." At the moment, it was something about shipping eyeglasses to the natives in Tahiti, the point being that the natives didn't wear glasses, so he felt he was in on the ground floor.

Enzo wanted to put the record straight. "Are you forgetting Roger Charles?"

Inky thought he meant her dentist and wanted to know what a man with a drill had to do with it. Rocky shushed her. Ruby ignored her.

Enzo continued with the lesson. "Shame on all of you. You claim to be devoted thespians and you don't remember Roger Charles?"

Ruby suddenly remembered. "Yes, yes. My mother worked with him. *When Blue Skies Turn Black and Oceans Don't Wave.* I was a child, of course. Barely remember. It starred Roger Charles and my mother, the late Vera Valk."

Enzo nodded. "And before that, Hymie Moscowitz." He loved knowing what he knew.

"From Moscowitz's Water-Beds?" Inky blurted out.

"Get a life," Ruby said, glaring at her.

"Hymie Moscowitz. The knife throwing act in the old days," Enzo said.

Jane knew more than she was letting on and was beginning to feel uncomfortable with the discussion of their boss like he was a patchwork quilt. To change the subject, she suggested the company do some warm-up exercises, perhaps some improvisations, while waiting for Glick/Roger/Hymie. Pandemonium broke out. Ruby was the most verbal. Who was this gofer, this assistant, to tell them what to do? She felt improvisations were a waste of time and that she didn't get where she was wondering who she was.

Trying not to be too controversial because while admiring Ruby, she was a little afraid of her, Jane explained that she was supposed to look after things when Glick Glickman wasn't there. Ruby finally relented and said she would do the scene in the shop with Enzo because she felt that was the one that needed the most work.

Jane exploded. "Sketch, not scene, Miss Valk. Scene implies a sub-division of an act of a play in which time is continuous and the setting is fixed. Sketch is a short play, often comic, forming part of a revue." She took her first breath since beginning the explanation.

Enzo was impressed. "Well-defined, Miss Smith." He threw out his first line to Ruby who wasn't ready. After checking her face in her hand mirror, she was ready.

Jane set it up. "Ruby's character is Lady Greene, with an 'e' and Enzo is a sales associate in a fancy London boutique. They both speak with upper Belgravia accents. That's British."

Ruby was annoyed. "We know all that."

Jane apologized. "Sorry. Just setting it up. Enzo, it's your line. Sorry."

Enzo began in character.

ENZO: Why didn't you come sooner, Lady Greene? We're sold out on the item you requested.

RUBY: I trust you are saying that with an E.

ENZO: There will be others. Shall I fix you a cup of tea?

RUBY: Not like him. His stripes. The way his fur fell.

ENZO: Perhaps you'd like a suede elephant? In gray.

RUBY: Lord Greene is partial to suede.

ENZO: Well, then, all's well that ends well.

RUBY: I just don't know. Oh, all right. Please send it.

ENZO: Super.

RUBY: That's awfully good of you, young man.

ENZO: Young girl, actually.

Out of character, Enzo said, "And end sketch. Laugh, laugh, laugh. I don't see any problems. It's funny. We know our lines."

Ruby was unsure about the material.

Rocky praised her. "You captured the emotion in a nutshell."

Ruby ignored his expressions of admiration and went on about the revue being nothing but an oral explosion and was bound to fail.

Inky went nuts over the fact she was appearing in a cough, according to the dictionary definition of an oral explosion. "*The Cough* starring that mad, mad, mad lady of comedy and blab, Inky Krabb. *The Cough* starring that funny, funny, funny man of television and stage, Rocky Rage. *The Cough* starring the multi-talented greatest Othello, Enzo Bordello." She had purposely left out Ruby Valk.

Jane was fuming. "It isn't a cough. It's a revue in words and movement based on a play based on an original short story, written by Glick Glickman, directed by Glick Glickman, and produced by Glick Glickman."

Ruby turned her back in a hostile gesture. "I refuse to be swept into litigation with the hired help." She chose to completely ignore the fact that they were all hired help.

Level-headed Enzo jumped in to diffuse the fast developing friction. He suggested a coffee break and instructed Jane, the gofer, to go for coffee. Jane was a little reluctant because she was worried that if Glick came in and she wasn't there, she would get in trouble. Rocky was starving and convinced Jane she had to go. Reluctantly, Jane gave in. Not wanting to get the order wrong, she wrote everything down, repeating the order as she wrote, and then summarizing it.

"Two black coffees, one with two sugars, one with no sugar. One regular with one sugar; one regular with five sugars. Four jelly doughnuts, one bran muffin, two cheese Danish pastries."

"Excellent, dear," said Enzo with encouragement.

"Now go," said Ruby. "Black, no sugar, no cream."

Jane went out the door, praying Glick wouldn't arrive while she was gone. She would get an extra coffee with cream and sugar the way he liked it, just in case he was there when she returned. For herself, she preferred a Diet Pepsi.

Rocky flopped down on the sofa, took a swift sneak sniff of Ruby's cape, and felt at peace. Enzo sat on one of the straight back chairs and quietly studied his script. Inky took out her mirror again and studied her face, hiding her displeasure with her reflection.

Ruby looked around at her co-actors and rolled her eyes upward. What had she got herself into? She lamented, "Singing, not singing; dancing, not dancing; sleeping, not sleeping; eating, not eating; drinking, not drinking; smoking, not smoking; loving, not loving. Such is my life these days. It's a life, I suppose. Of course, it is." Her tone was soft and sweet as warm maple syrup. She knew how to deliver a line.

Rocky was more in love with her now than he had been a minute before. "That is beautiful. A song without music. You'll stop the show."

Ruby snapped at him, "Are you crazy? You think Glick wrote that? That's all me. My soul bared."

"Personally, I like my sole grilled." Inky quipped, positive she had delivered the cleverest line of the century.

Ignoring Inky, Rocky said, "Seriously, Ruby, that could be straight out of Tennessee Williams."

Without skipping a beat, Inky came back with, "That won't even be compared to Esther Williams."

Taking his eyes off his script, Enzo said, "Now there's a masterpiece of all time."

Completing misunderstanding, Ruby said, "She wasn't that great."

"Not Esther, you fool. Tennessee," Inky corrected.

Caught up in the moment, Ruby said, "I played in a touring company of *Streetcar*."

"And what did you base your Stanley Kowalski on?" asked Inky.

Ruby was fuming. "You insane person. I played Blanche Dubois."

"Before your nervous breakdown or after?" asked Inky innocently.

Before this exchange ended in a cat fight, Enzo stepped in and broke it up. Ruby took this as an opportunity to speak privately to him. She asked if she could have a word, but he turned her down, saying that he had to study his lines.

Ruby felt desperate. To no one in particular, but meaning Enzo, she said, "I love him so. Last Sunday was the best day of my life. He came over to rehearse. We argued about the script. We watched *Clockwork Orange*. Then we talked and talked about the Mafia, the CIA, about guns and war, and all the starvation in the world. I've never felt such total harmony with another human being." Her monologue was heartfelt. Too bad the critics weren't there.

Inky knew what she meant. She, too, loved someone. And that someone was in love with someone else. Damn that Ruby. Inky knew her emotional life with Rocky was based only on their work, but still, she hoped. Yesterday, she had nearly fainted after doing the sketch about Sandra's pregnancy. Rocky brought her a glass of water and told her to unzip her jeans so she could breathe. No matter how much she deeply wanted him, she knew the glass of water wasn't personal. He would have done it for anyone in denim. He was that kind of a guy.

Ruby started grumbling and rambling again. First, it was something about coming back from the coast for this fiasco that didn't have a final script and was opening in a week. "At least when you're out of work in Los Angeles, you can work on your tan."

Then she got onto Inky. "And you. Change your name. Inky Krabb. What is that? She claims it's her real name based on her initials. I. N. K. Irene Nancy Krabb; hence the Inky. Give me a break!"

"It's true," Inky said defensively. "That is my name. Besides, it's none of your darn business."

"Oh, *darn* is it?"

"Since we're playing true confessions," Enzo said, in a mellow mood, "I've always said I was named after my aunt who brought me up. Mildred Bordello. I've never told this to anyone. Her name was Mildred Clodhopper. She ran a bordello."

After a moment, during which Enzo was thinking about Enzo and everyone else was thinking about his aunt's bordello, he said, "Do you people remember that wonderful show where I made my entrance on the wings of an angel? *Rudolf of Sardinia.*"

Rocky knew the back story. "If I recall correctly, you made your exit three seconds later through the proscenium arch into an ambulance."

"It was my first break," Enzo said, not intending the double meaning.

Rocky and Inky together imitated a drum roll. "Boom. Boom." But they both knew Enzo could never be the comedian. His delivery was always just a hair off.

Gofer Jane Smith returned carrying a large paper sack with the food and a carton with the coffees. Being slightly clumsy, she tripped over her own feet on her entrance. It was a most unfortunate turn of events. Coffee, doughnuts, pastries, etcetera went spilling onto the floor. Everyone watched while she got down on her hands and knees and tried to salvage some of the goods, apologizing, saying she would go out again. Holding up a soggy piece of paper, she reassured the others she still had the list.

Ruby was furious. "Am I now going to be reduced to carrying my own thermos?"

Rocky didn't want Ruby to ever be upset about anything. To appease her, he offered the tidbit that Ginger Rogers brought her own bottled water to the theatre when she performed. Not wanting to be upstaged by anyone, Inky threw in that it was a known fact that Carol Channing carried her own food to parties in a bowling bag.

Jane, who had been working on the floor diligently, held up a coffee. "Here's one."

Inky took it and handed it to Rocky. Rocky took it and handed it to Ruby. Ruby took it and handed it to Enzo. Enzo took it and drank it.

Feeling refreshed, Enzo suggested they do some rehearsing. Jane wanted to know if she should go for more coffee. Everyone ignored her. Ruby grabbed her things and headed for the door saying she was absolutely leaving; only to be physically blocked by Jane's body. Ruby told her to be more careful and blasted out something about wanting to know where Glick had found her. All eyes were now on Jane. And all ears were at the ready.

Jane hesitated, not sure how much should be said. Where did Glick find her? She wasn't an orphan left on church steps somewhere. She cleared her throat and slowly began. "Mr. Glickman had a florist business for a couple of years. You know, after the theatre business dried up. He had a dog, too. I was working as a temp for the director of a funeral home. Benny Klingman Funerals. It was my first job after...after. Never mind that." She paused before continuing, hoping the 'after' hadn't carved an opening into her secret life. "Anyway, Mr. Glickman did all the floral arrangements. He was known for his special arrangements in black. One time he ran out of spray. He would spray the flowers. He told me to go out and buy a can. So I did. I paid ninety cents. When I got back, he gave me five dollars and said to keep the change, because you see, up to that time, he was paying a dollar a can. I saved him ten cents. And that's when he hired me to work for him."

There was silence from the stunned group.

Jane continued, "The dog's name was Sandy Mathieson O'Reilly Goldstein. He died. He didn't suffer. He just died. In his sleep. It was an elaborate funeral. And I've worked for him ever since. For Glick Glickman, not the dog, but I guess you realized that, I guess."

When Ruby could find her voice after that riveting bit of information, she spewed out, "My first job in the theatre in four years, and I'm tied up with a mortician's temp."

Inky told her not to worry, that it would be subtitled. Jane burst into tears and ran off crying, presumably to the ladies room.

"That girl is way too high strung to be in the theatre," Ruby said.

Inky understood. "She loves someone who doesn't love her." She burst into tears and ran off crying, also in the direction of the ladies room.

For reasons only she understood, Ruby burst into tears and ran off towards the ladies room.

Rocky bowed his head to Enzo, explained he had low blood sugar and had to get some food. He ran straight for the prop room.

Enzo was thrilled. Alone at last with his true love, he kissed his hand, bowed slowly to the universe, said his silent thank you's, and strutted off grandly to the gent's. Talk about clearing a room…

As they say in show biz, he was the master.

6

ENTER GLICK, HYMIE, ROGER

MISS SMITH, WHERE THE HELL ARE YOU?" yelled the entrepreneur, theatrical producer, director, playwright, Glick Glickman aka Hymie Moskowitz, knife thrower extraordinaire aka Roger Charles, actor even more extraordinaire. Upon entering an empty rehearsal studio, he sounded like an ensnared lion in the wild. To say he was surprised would be putting it below mildly. Fast-talking, brash, quick-witted Glick Glickman laid his huge, worn, brown leather briefcase on the table/desk and for one of the very few times in his life was at a loss for words. Not only because the company appeared to be missing, but because he was in serious trouble. The dough he thought he had, he didn't have. Backers, schmackers. Angels. A man's whole life, whole career, is crushed with one word. Two lousy syllables. EN—O. No. That's how it worked in the business of show. No dough, no show.

He sat on a prop chair at the table. He leaned forward and buried his face in his hands. Leaning forward had been a mistake. The hair on his head moved out of place and had to be adjusted. The rug made his scalp itch, his head was always hot, and the damned thing never stayed on straight. He hated it. But he hated his bald scalp more.

He was in trouble. He couldn't postpone the opening while he tried to find the money elsewhere because he had paid a non-refundable fee to the theatre to open on a certain date. Press releases were out. He was doomed. And where was his cast? You'd think they'd be grateful to be working again in a real show. This was the chance to revive Broadway, for chrissakes. He had to think. He wasn't seeing the full picture. He should know how to fix this problem, but he was struggling to find an answer.

He started to pace. If he could get his four actors to continue to rehearse while he looked for the finances, that might be one solution. Maybe he wouldn't tell them the truth. Maybe that wasn't such a good idea. Maybe Jane could explain it to them. Where was she? All of them? It was eleven-fifteen o'clock in the morning. Their call was for ten.

"SMITH," he bellowed.

After five or six hollered "Smiths," Jane came sheepishly out of the ladies room and apologized for not being there.

"Never mind. You are all late. Something I won't have in the the-a-ter." No one pronounced words in quite the same way as Glick Glickman.

Jane quickly explained they were all there, that he was the late one; therefore, they took an early lunch break.

"Are you contradicting the man who pays you?" Still pacing, Glick, ever the director, ever the leader, ever the guru, lost in thought, fingered his upper lip. "Maybe I'll grow a moustache. Look what it did for Hitler." He eyed Jane's hair. "Fuses again?"

Jane nodded. She waited. It was all she could do when he paced. He once said she was his co-pilot. What did the mean? Could she ever be a woman to him? The light would go out in the world if she couldn't take notes for him, type his memos, shine his shoes, sharpen his pencils, carry his box of Kleenex, cancel his hotel reservations, page him in restaurants to impress people, do his laundry, pick up his dry cleaning.

"Hello? Jane Smith, come in. Listen. I had it right here." Glick held out his left hand, palm up. "I can make it work. I can taste it. Don't leave me, Jane. I could get the money just like that." He snapped his fingers. "It's that skinny Inky Krabb. Her chest is like two raisins on an ironing board. And she can't sing."

His voice, his magnificent, rich gravel voice with just a smattering of honey mixed in, took Jane out of her reverie. "But it isn't a musical."

"And why do you think it isn't a musical? A musical, I could get the money."

Jane knew a little about show biz and told him that Inky Krabb was a comedienne. She didn't have to sing good. She was funny. The secret love of her life looked so forlorn. "You had the money. You can get it again," Jane said, hoping to boost his spirits.

For Glick this was last chance saloon. If he didn't get this show on, the business was finished for good. Kaput. He'd have to call off his life. And then it came to him. His eyes glazed over as they always did when he had a new idea. "Fat Chat," he uttered. "I know it's supposed to be Fat Cat, but I like my name better."

"Where? I hate cats," Jane squirmed, looking around. "When I was a kid, I had a book called *Fraidy Cat*. I walked around with it under my arm. I was too afraid to read it."

In his own world now, he said, "I heard he got out a few days ago. He must have money stashed away. His number's in my book. Go. Fetch," Glick said, snapping his fingers.

Jane found Glick's private book of numbers in his briefcase and started turning the pages. She turned to the C's, but there was no Cat or Chat. She asked, "Under C?"

"Huh? F. I told you a million times, we file by first name

only on account of a lot of my associates do not reveal their last names."

Jane was skeptical and wondered if Mister Cat/Chat was still alive. She'd heard terrible things can happen to people inside the big house. She questioned Glick about it.

"I got a six year old nephew doesn't ask as many questions. Unfortunately, it's illegal to employ him."

Jane laughed inwardly. Just another brilliant retort from her hero. She continued to look for Fat's number.

Glick punched in a number on his cell. After a brief preliminary chit chat with his bookie about the weather, Glick explained his dilemma. "Listen, I got five million dollars tied up in a Hong Kong account. All I need is ninety-nine grand to get my new Broadway show off the ground. I had the dough, but…hello? How do you like that bum. He hung up on me."

Jane thought she knew a little about finance and told him that if he had five million dollars in a Hong Kong bank, all he had to do was instruct them to transfer the funds from the current account to a deposit account, and the bank would lend him the ninety-nine thousand.

Glick couldn't believe what he was hearing. "Don't be cute. Where would I have five million bucks in Hong Kong? Last year I got the Hong Kong flu. Sick as a dog. Two hundred and ten temperature and that's what I know from Hong Kong. I hate those Chinks." He grabbed the well-used address book out of Jane's hands and started flipping through the pages.

"Why don't you keep his number in your contacts?" Jane asked.

He looked at her blankly.

"On your cell phone. There's a place. I could show you."

Still looking for the F's, he reminded her that certain numbers for security reasons could not be kept in that manner. "Got it. Under E. I forgot. A secret code." He punched in the number and never one to waste a minute, while he waited, he let his brain run wild.

Theatre was at its finest when it portrayed life. What did people want? Excitement. Sex. Violence. That was it. *A Little Revue* was too mild. He'd bring back the old act. The sexiest and most violent and most exciting of them all. Hymie Moscowitz. King of the Knife. King of the Blindfold. What took him so long to figure it out? Okay, so he wasn't perfect. If Christ was so perfect, he would've established new track and field records. Fat Cat's voice on the other end of the phone came on, but it was voice mail. That didn't deter Glick.

"Fat? I hope you haven't lost any weight. Just kidding. G.G. here. Have I got a deal for you!" Glick explained about the show without really explaining and told Fat Cat to be at the rehearsal studio that night at five minutes of eight. He only hoped he got the message. You could never be sure with answering machines and voice mail. It was a new world of non-communication via technology which was a very difficult world for the man who prized himself to be the face to face master communicator.

Glick snapped his phone shut and pulled out a blindfold and a stubby lethal looking dagger from his briefcase. He held the blindfold out for Jane. She took it and slipped the elastic part around her head so that it covered her eyes.

"Not yours. Mine!" he shouted. "I'll be lucky I don't get a coronary from you."

Jane took off the blindfold and placed it around Glick's eyes. She tested that he couldn't see by waving her hand up and down in front of his face. She turned him around and around and around.

He could feel the old adrenalin pumping through his entire body. He told her to stop the turning. "Stand over there." He pointed somewhere.

"Where?" Jane asked. She had been through a lot with him over the years, but this was a new development. It kind of thrilled her.

"How should I know? I can't see. Against a wall somewhere." He could hear her footsteps. "Are you there?"

"I'm here, G.G.," she said clearly as if they were in a prisoner of war camp, not that she'd ever been in one, and their lives depended on her answer.

Glick prepared by taking a deep breath. He held the sharp knife in his fingers, aimed, held it a second or two, and then with a swift twist of the wrist, hurled the stabbing weapon at Jane. It was buried in the wall next to her head. A loud thud followed. Slightly trembling, Glick, as Hymie, removed his blindfold with a dramatic hand movement. Always the showman. Jane's body lay on the floor in a gnarled position. Glick stood over her and waited. Perhaps not dead; perhaps just in shock.

Slowly, Jane opened her eyes. The first thing she saw was the love of her life looking down at her. Looking up at him, she said meekly, "You missed."

Glick broke out in a big grin and threw his hands in the air. YES! The knife was exactly where it was supposed to be. The audience will be waiting for him to hit his target, but he'll miss every time. The act was back. He'll line up Enzo, Ruby, Rocky, and Inky. The only piece of cloth on the stage will be his blindfold; some bits and pieces for the actors like those modesty pieces they do in the movies in nude scenes. He'd get all the backing he needed. He'd have a real show. He hadn't lost his touch. He, single-handedly, would bring p-zzazz back to Broadway. It had come to him in a flash.

"AND IT TOOK GOD *SIX* DAYS," he cried out to the universe.

7

THE BACKER'S AUDITION

At ten minutes to eight that night, the small company was lined up in costume, albeit flimsy, but still covering the essential body parts that should be covered. They were not happy about it, but ready to perform the backer's audition as their only hope.

Fat Cat hadn't been changed by his stint in prison. He was as greasy and sleazy as ever. Fat? He was wire thin. No one knew his exact origins or, for that matter, his real name, or his age, or why he was called Fat Cat. He could have been from anywhere in the world. He was definitely interested in putting money into a show headed for Broadway that could possibly be the revival of the entire New York theatre, not to mention his reputation. He admitted to never having seen a play on Broadway, off Broadway, or off-off Broadway. In fact, he had never seen a live stage production. His high school stressed woodworking and farming. It was Glick's good luck that Fat Cat had done a heist, got caught, done a stretch inside, but, and here was the good part, they never found the stash. Fat Cat saw this as an opportunity to add some interest to his principal, the whereabouts of which still had not been revealed. Glick wasn't sure there really was any money, but he was in a bind and had nothing else.

That's how he operated. With a wing and a prayer. Somehow, it always worked out. Well, not always.

Scantily clad, Ruby Valk, Enzo Bordello, Inky Krabb, and Rocky Rage were lined up waiting for the cue to begin. They were embarrassed, but being professionals, they kept it all inside. When you needed work, you did crazy things, things you might never otherwise have done.

In full costume that included black flowing pants, a puffy white blouse, a red sash, Glick as Hymie was prepared to convince Fat Cat to invest in the show.

"Did I tell a lie, Fat? Huh? It's a winner. Sex. Just look at those costumes. Violence. Look at these knives." He held up four short lethal daggers. He could feel the tingling in his bones. Just like the old days. Sex and violence. A small company, not those huge casts that put Broadway out of business. "You'll never have to knock off another liquor store, Fat. This show could run forever. You'll see your money double in no time. Triple." Glick was practically foaming at the mouth. "Hymie Moscowitz is back!"

His short fuse about to explode, Fat Cat threatened, "You're gonna be the *late* Hymie Moscowitz if you don't stop yappin.'"

In a cute little short white satin skirt, a red sequined halter top, and white high heeled shoes, her hair piled high on her head, Jane placed the blindfold around Glick's eyes the way they had rehearsed. Glick/Hymie held the daggers in his fingers, and with the agility of a young artiste, he aimed at his targets and flung the knives. One-two-three-four. Bop-bop-bop-bop. He missed every time. He removed the blindfold with a grand gesture, held it up with one arm raised to the ceiling, took his bow. Jane nearly fainted again. Inky, Rocky, Enzo, and Ruby were beyond fainting. They were glad to be breathing. It was a sure sign they were still alive.

Fat Cat leapt off the chair. "You must take me for some kind of chump. You missed. Four times, you missed."

Glick was desperate. "You want longer knives? I can get longer knives."

"No one pulls a fast one over Fat Cat. Where would I be if I missed my targets every time I aimed? Dead. That's where I'd be."

Glick explained that this was entertainment. He was supposed to miss. That was the point. The audience was waiting for him to hit, but he misses. He's blindfolded.

Fat Cat had a different take on the matter. "You got lousy aim that's your trouble. How long do you think that's gonna hold an audience? The show'll close before intermission," he ranted and raved beyond reason.

And then it came to Glick. "Wait a minute. Wait a sec. Let me understand. You'll put up the dough if, instead of missing, I hit?"

"Bullseye!"

"Bloodshed. That's the word I couldn't think of. Reality theatre. The title will be, *Aim to Kill*. Now there's a show. It'll be the first ever. Real live death on stage every night plus two matinees."

Breathing hard, Fat Cat was in the spirit now as he listened to Glick.

With great relish, Glick went on. "A cast of millions. Four at a time. Nobody'll ever be out of work. Actors' Equity will give me an award; maybe name a scholarship after me."

That was it for Ruby. That did it. She said she was going to see her lawyer. Inky said to count her out. Rocky wondered if it was too late in life to train to be a great chef, and Enzo said he'd have to return to the idiot box. At least there, when you got stabbed, they used ketchup.

Glick had to think fast. He couldn't lose his opening cast. He told them they had the money; that the show could open in a week. Their careers would bloom once again.

"Bloom? We'll all be dead," Rocky said, trembling.

Referring to Fat sleaze ball Cat, Ruby said, "He may have the cash flow, but I like my blood to flow, and I don't mean all over the stage, thank you very much." She started to gather her belongings and as she was stuffing them in her bag, she added, "Glickman, there aren't enough actors in the world for the kind of success you're talking about."

"My hands are tied," Glick said, trying to sound convincing. "I'm dealing with a hardened crim-er-businessman here. We all know he's a little *meshugah*, but so what?"

Fat Cat said firmly, "I ain't hangin' 'round here all night. Take it or leave it. Ninety-nine K give or take."

Ruby said she was out of there, but didn't move. Rocky said he was gone, but didn't move. Inky said she was out, but didn't move. Enzo said he was right behind them, but didn't move. Their physical state had a name. Frozen with fear. Or it could simply have been the aforementioned ninety-nine thousand dollars, 'K' meaning thousand. Maybe there was a way to fake the knives not to mention their deaths.

Glick began his pep talk. "Come on, kids, we'll just be giving the public what they want. They see it on television, now they can see it in the flesh."

Fat Cat was dwelling on the fact he'd been called crazy and in another language yet. He was raging with fury. No one called him crazy. He grabbed his revolver from inside his coat. No one saw it coming. The screams from Ruby, Inky, Rocky, and Enzo could have been heard down the block. Fat was taking aim at Glick. In a flash, Jane flung herself in front of her secret love. Fat Cat pulled the trigger. There was a loud click. He looked at the gun. Jane looked down at the front of her body. She was still upright. There wasn't any blood. Humiliated, Fat Cat ran out of the studio declaring that they hadn't seen the last of him.

Not immediately grasping the situation, Glick thought he'd been shot and dropped to the ground pulling Jane with him. "*Et tu?*"

Led by Enzo, the company including Ruby, Inky, and Rocky broke into a chorus of lament, as in a Greek chorus.

> *O, sight for all the world to see*
> *Most terrible, O suffering*
> *Of all mine eyes have seen most horrible*
> *Alas, what fury?*
> *What evil spirits?*
> *All for a show*
> *Without the dough*
> *Glick Glickman, Hymie Moscowitz, Roger Charles*
> *O, terror*
> *Better wert thou dead*
> *Than living in a box*
> *Somewhere under a bridge.*

Cradling Glick in her arms, Jane was so overwhelmed with emotion, she couldn't speak. With his rugged and raw looks and charm and talent and charisma, he could have had anybody's arms, but he chose hers. She was bound to him. And she knew, the way you knew something like that, he felt something for her, too, even though he once said she had a profile like a demented carrot.

Glick's voice cracked when he finally spoke. "You saved my life, Jane Smith."

"There weren't any bullets in the gun."

"But who knew? There could have been," he said.

Having seen enough, Ruby headed for the door, followed by Rocky, Inky, and Enzo. Glick extricated himself from Jane's arms and crawled after them. "Go. Who cares? I'll do a one-man show. I'll get the money. You're all has-beens. Without me, you're nothing. You know that old man who drags himself around Times Square with that banner?

'Eating lentils and sitting is bad for society.' That's you people without me."

Just as the quartet was about to leave, Jane rushed over, blocking their exit, shouting for them not to go because she had something important to tell them. She pulled a telegram out of her pocket and waved it in front of them. "The show can go on. Look here. I have the money. I can back the show."

There were groans from everyone with remarks like 'delusions of grandeur' and 'the pace of show business has finally got her.' Jane begged them to listen. She told them she received the telegram that afternoon, but with all the excitement, forgot about it. She asked them all to sit down so she could explain. More intrigued than for any other reason, the company and Glick did as they were told.

Jane began. "I've sat back and done what I was told, getting in the way mostly, but now, here is something I can do. I have the money."

Money? Glick never was one to pass up an opportunity to raise the almighty dollar. Maybe the kid had something. He was willing to listen. "Okay, Jane Smith, go ahead. Speak."

"That's just it. I'm not Jane Smith."

8

ANGEL DAPHNE

My real name is Daphne Sockafeller."

You could have heard a pin drop on the cement floor. That's how quiet it was; that is, before the loud gasps. Really loud.

"Listen. It's all here." Jane took the telegram out of her pocket and waved it at them.

"Not *the* Daphne Sockafeller?" Ruby and Inky said in unison.

Enzo knew the name. "Daughter of the real estate mogul and philanthropist Ernest Sockafeller?"

"Niece," Jane quickly corrected him.

"Ernest Sockafeller is your uncle?" Glick was astounded. He thought he knew everything about her.

"Was," Jane clarified. "He died two and a half months ago. The Executors of the Estate didn't know how to get in touch with me. He left me everything."

There was a quick silent group calculation. It had to be billions.

"Yes, billions," she said, reading their collective minds.

There was suddenly a lot of interest in Jane/Daphne. A lot of questions. Like, why was she working as a temp and then a gofer when she had all that?

And for the first time, Jane revealed her true identity. "Uncle Ernest was appointed my legal guardian when my parents were killed in a plane crash. I was five months old. I was brought up in a big house, a mansion really, with lots of servants. I never had to do anything for myself."

Of course, that explained why she didn't have any skills. Why she couldn't go out and bring back coffee and doughnuts without the paper sack crashing to the floor.

"As I got older, Uncle Ernest's feelings became more than an uncle for a niece. Terrified of his attentions, I ran away. You know the rest. The funeral home temp job. Meeting Glick Glickman." Jane handed Glick the telegram.

He studied it. Dear Jane. So uncomplicated. So rich. She had the money now and wanted to produce the show.

"And I can still be your assistant. Nothing has changed." To reinforce her words, she put on her glasses.

But Glick knew everything had changed. What was he to do? He was an entrepreneur. She had been his assistant. Sometimes things didn't work out; sometimes they did. You just had to ride the waves. Wanting to talk to Jane alone, he dismissed the company, telling them to get a good night's rest and be back the next morning at ten.

One by one, each embraced Jane and congratulated Glick, and spontaneously broke into a song vaguely sounding like the tune, *For She's a Jolly Good Fellow.*

Glick was antsy to get on with the Jane/Daphne meeting. "This ain't a remake of *Good News* with June and Peter. Go home, kids. I got a show to rewrite. Tomorrow morning, ten o'clock in the morning, sharp, on time, ten."

Funny what money can do, Jane thought. The company had actually hugged her and gave her thumbs up and cheered her. They had never hugged her before. Or sung to her. It had been a day of firsts.

"Take a memo, Miss Jane Smith and/or Daphne Sockafeller."

"You can call me Jane or Daphne. Just call me." She laughed at what she thought was an original joke.

"Not new and not particularly funny. Listen. New subject. On account of people saying they are whom, or who, they turn out not to be, from now on, there will be a fine for any changes of names on contracts, playbills, programs, invitations, and handouts."

Jane wasn't taking notes as she had in the past. During his speech, she slowly took off her glasses and took the clip out of her now bone dry hair. With her fingers, she fluffed out the thick and curly brunette locks that fell nearly to her shoulders.

Glick was somewhat in awe of this new creature before him. Suddenly, she was more than the silly temp who once saved him a dime on a can of spray. She was, and he found this hard to admit, a woman. And when all the greasepaint came off, he was a man. She was beautiful without her notepad, pencil, and glasses. He studied her. Her eyes were green. He never realized that. Green was his favorite color. It made a nice combination. Green for eyes. Green for money.

Jane knew that look. She'd seen it in movies a million times. Her secret love didn't have to be a secret anymore. Her eyes, maybe her hair, maybe her money had won him over. He indicated for her to sit beside him on the sofa. And then he shared something with her that he had never told anyone before.

"I was five or six. I was in bed sleeping, but I wasn't sleeping. My mother came in after they'd been out for the evening, leaned down, and kissed me. She still had on her fur coat. There are two things I always remember: the cold fur against my cheek and her smell."

Jane had no idea why he would be telling her this now. Perhaps the idea of all that money loosened his tongue. She looked at him blankly. This was a different Glick Glickman.

Glick picked up her thought. It was a kind of shorthand they had between them. "I found out when I got older it wasn't real fur. We never had genuine anything. All those years, I thought it was because we were poor."

Jane knew exactly what he meant. "It was for humane reasons, not because your folks were poor. Money doesn't mean furs and leather and all that expensive stuff."

"I know," Glick said. "Faux is good." He wanted to swim in her green eyes that were like that Mediterranean Sea off the coast of Greece at sunrise poster he once saw in a travel agency window.

"Faux is good," she repeated.

"I said that." Wanting to tell her something and thinking it would be easier for her if he wasn't looking directly at her, he turned his head away. "So you never knew your mother or father. That must have been rough."

She lowered her voice. "You don't miss what you never had."

He didn't want to dwell on an unpleasant memory. He did what he did best. He lightened up the conversation. "Well, Jane Smith, so you're one of those 'eiresses. You're gonna be different now."

"Different? I don't think so," she said. "I grew up with money. Then I didn't have it because I didn't know I had it. Now I have it again. And I know I have it. So it's not so different. Of all people, you would understand that."

Here was Glick's favorite subject. Money. He knew about money. What it can do and what the lack of it can't do. There were only two things money couldn't buy. Money couldn't buy back yesterday, and money couldn't buy class. Glick knew that no matter how much money he'd accumulate, and from time to time, he did accumulate it, it could never make him a class act. The thorn in his side. So he invented Roger Charles. An actor had class. In the eyes of the world, just the name Roger Charles gave him class. Hooray for show business. Without it, he was just that insecure little kid waiting for his parents to come home and kiss him goodnight.

Jane followed her impulse, leaned over, and kissed him smack on the mouth.

The gesture surprised him. And he wasn't easily surprised. "What's that for?" he asked, even though he had an idea.

"You know what that's for," she said coyly. "I saw you had a certain look on your face. I've never seen that look before except when you were pleased you closed a deal."

"Ah, yes. I am familiar with that look of mine."

In her most business-like voice Jane said, "We have a deal?"

He had prayed for money. He didn't specify where it was going to get it from. He didn't care. "Tell ya what. I'll take you out for a bite, and we can talk."

Jane had a better idea. "Why don't I fix us something at my place? We can work there."

"Your landlord finally fixed the leak in the roof?"

"I did," Jane said with great pride.

Oh brother, Glick thought. He knew what was coming next. She had the dough. She owned him. She would want to direct, produce, re-write, and probably star even though she never acted a day in her life. Or maybe she had. Maybe she hadn't dropped that other shoe yet. Here it was in the flesh, that old show biz saying, 'Money bags calls the tune.' To tell the truth, he wasn't sure how he felt about that. Up to now, rain or shine, calm or stormy weather, he'd always been the captain.

9

METAMORPHOSIS

Back at her place, Jane served sumptuous tuna sandwiches on rye bread with Dijon mustard, Hellmann's mayonnaise, and Heinz ketchup. It was the way he liked his sandwiches. Whether it was tuna, ham, chicken, bologna, salami, roast beef, or corned beef. It had to have mustard, mayonnaise, and ketchup, and it had to be on rye bread. And she knew that. He couldn't get over it. Daphne Sockafeller was serving him a sandwich. Someone that rich working for him, serving him. It was like...like Donald Trump's daughter working for four dollars an hour in a cookie factory.

While sipping her Pepsi, she told him, "It was fun not knowing who you were going to be next. I guess that should be present tense. I never met anyone like you."

"Look who's talking about an identity crisis," he said. "You're a person of dual identity." He took a large bite of his sandwich. "This is good." After a beat, he added, "That's the reason my first wife left me." Since they were baring their souls, he figured there was no harm in telling her.

"Because of tuna?" This was news.

"Not because of tuna."

"You said your first wife. How many times have you been married?" Not that it mattered to her.

Glick explained, "Just once. A long time ago. I always say it that way. Not planning on any others. We were from the same neighborhood. It's how it was done then. You got married and you went into your father-in-law's business. He owned a fleet of taxicabs. A good business, but it wasn't me. The marriage didn't last long. I needed to taxi down a different road."

"The road less traveled," she said, quoting her favorite poet, Robert Frost.

Glick thought it was a little late in the day for philosophy, but he was fascinated by this new personage that had emerged who had been in his life as one thing and now had changed into another.

Good title for something. *The Metamorphosis.*

Into a very lucrative other. God bless telegrams. Daphne Jane Smith Sockafeller not only had the goods he needed for the show, she was a damned good looker, and she could put together a sandwich the way he liked it. It was time to talk business. He tuned in to her chatter, having no idea what she was saying.

Jane's voice droned on. "See what I mean? It is my belief people come into your life for a reason. Some power of energy put me in your path, and the wondrous part is you don't have to believe it for it to happen. It just does."

Glick was uncomfortable. "Okay, this is getting a little heavy. New topic."

"You're laughing at me."

He reassured her that she was not in the least funny.

Thoroughly offended at his remark, she pouted.

"Hey, not everybody can be a comedian. Don't get a complex about it. You got other attributes that others don't have. Enough chit chat. We got a show to revise."

"No more knives and blindfolds?"

"Hymie Moscowitz has left the stage."

Imitating Glick's voice, with great jubilance, she announced, "*The Daphne Sockafeller Revue.*"

"Oish," he let out air through his back teeth which were clenched. "It doesn't exactly have a flow to it, but what the hell?" He raised his arms in a triumphant gesture. Glick knew when to give in. She had what he needed. It was that simple. Who knew the temp would turn into an angel. His angel.

"With you and me, we don't need the usual legal documents, do we? A handshake?" She put out her hand.

"My word is my bond. Come here."

Jane and or Daphne went into his outstretched arms like a bunch of bananas caressing her. Being practically a vegetarian who ate meat sometimes, she loved the feeling. Whoever said money didn't buy happiness never had any money.

The show would go on. Broadway would have the revival of a lifetime. Glick Glickman would be cited in theatre history books and talked about in theatre schools all over the country. Maybe the world. Once again, he'd landed in butter. It wasn't *how* you got there; it was that you got there. Even with this sure thing, he had a back-up plan. He didn't always follow his own advice. If this show didn't work, if he couldn't get Broadway back on its feet, and he was savvy enough to know that that could happen, he would be heading south to that joint he knew about in Florida for early retirement. Not so early, if you peeked under all the skin lifts he'd had done over the years. In private, he referred to himself as the male Joan Rivers.

He knew in his bones that this theatre project was last chance saloon. He had to take the shot. If this venture didn't work out, his heart couldn't take another flop. And his vigor was waning. He just wouldn't have the energy to start again. The business had changed. Why go to the theatre?

Folks could get all the entertainment they wanted on their hand-held phones.

What Jane didn't realize, by putting all her capital into the show, she could lose all her capital. He didn't want to be around to pick up the pieces. If it was a hit…and why wouldn't it be…he was Glick Glickman…but then, she would have control. If it was a flop, there was no need to mention he would probably have no choice but to disappear. Next to going into the witness protection program, the place in Florida would be his best choice. West Palm Acres. He had a friend who died there. But that's another story. In God's waiting room, he could be anonymous living out his so-called golden years in relative comfort. He'd have enough with social security and the modest nest egg he'd quietly accumulated over the years. If he'd learned anything in his checkered career, it was always to have a Plan B.

10

YOU'RE NEVER ALONE WITH SCHIZOPHRENIA

Having completed his duties of the morning, Jon Sullivan went to his room to freshen up before going to the staff dining area for his lunch break. Two months and one week had gone by since his arrival at West Palm Acres. To his surprise, to his dismay, he was still there. Originally, he thought it would be four weeks maximum before he'd be back working in New York. His agent told him there was nothing for him right now, to stay at West Palm Acres and be happy he had any kind of job at all. It wasn't as if he was totally unhappy. All in all, it wasn't a bad gig. In fact, he had become quite philosophical about his employment at West Palm Acres. He was of the opinion that everything happened for a reason. Even if he didn't know why, he was meant to meet these folks. They were intelligent and funny who, through good genes or good luck, had lived long enough to become what society labeled 'senior citizens.' He thought of his parents and made a mental note to phone them that evening.

Jon's job had been the pilot for a new program. He wondered if anyone was healthier as a result of the medication reminder. He probably would never know. It was deemed a success by the powers that be and the upshot was that other retirement communities were in the throes of setting up a similar routine. All he knew was he was living in decent digs, had a warm place to sleep, ate regularly, and was meeting some nice people.

And now, a new experiment was being looked into. Actually, the idea was Jon's. Because many elderly folks had insomnia, sleep sitters were being considered. A sitter would stay with the resident as long as it took for the person to fall asleep. It might involve reading to them, serving them warm milk, or just talking. It was early days, so the details hadn't been worked out yet. West Palm Acres would once again be the test community. Jon didn't know if they would be expecting him to launch the program as the first sleep sitter. He wasn't sure he even wanted to do it. Anyway, as it turned out, all the speculation was just that. It didn't happen. People would have to fall asleep on their own.

When he told his colleagues back in New York what he was doing, they were astonished that he could have sunk so low. Low? No, not low. Jon wondered if there wasn't a little jealousy involved. Not only had he taken to the people, but there was an actual theatre on the property where shows were booked to entertain the residents. Big names came in regularly. Steve Lawrence and Eydie Gorme had made their comeback at West Palm Acres and claimed their careers had been revived as a result of playing the retirement communities in Florida.

Most of all and most importantly, Jon was becoming quite fond of the folks and especially his tightly knit group. Oscar Shapiro and Harry Goldberg came up with unbelievably funny stuff, bringing to mind those two characters, Statler and Waldorf, from the Muppet Show. Valeska Bernhart was old Hollywood, an era the likes of which would never be seen again. She was warm and funny and not the least bit stuck-up. And Glick Glickman was Mister Show Business. He was vaudeville, television, and theatre rolled into one, not to mention his other talents. The mourning period for his old life eventually played itself out. He was too much of a people person to remain in isolation. He had turned out to be a real *mensch*, meaning a good person.

It had been a stormy start for Valeska and Glick. Her comment to Harry Goldberg when he told her Glick Glickman was living next door to her was, "Glick who?" She pretended not to know who he was. They had never met, but she knew of him. "Some fly by night pseudo impresario like so many today," she said through the side of her mouth.

"He's the genuine article." Harry raised his right hand to heaven. "I swear."

"A real pseudo, you mean?" She refused to believe Glick Glickman would be at West Palm Acres, completely ignoring the fact that *she* was there.

When Glick was told by Jon that Valeska Bernhart was in the apartment next to his, he remarked, "Can't be. She died years ago. I saw it on *Entertainment Tonight*."

Jon didn't push the point. He figured they would soon meet.

And then the inevitable happened. They ran into one another one afternoon while waiting for the elevator. They politely nodded without exchanging a word. The next time they saw one another, they were seated in the dining room at adjacent tables. The penny dropped and this time, Glick took a closer look. In fact, he did a double take.

He blurted out, "You're not dead." He had never learned to filter his thoughts.

"No, I guess not. And you are?" she said, pretending not to know who he was, 'pretending' being the operative word, because she knew. She also knew that the brash newcomer to West Palm Acres intrigued the hell out of her. Voices turned her on. No one sounded like he did. Maybe the late Wallace Beery mixed in with a little Walter Huston all those years ago. But there was nobody now. Glick Glickman was a one-off.

Taking her at her word, or playing along, he asked, "Does the name Hymie Moscowitz mean anything?" He waited.

"Let me see. Oh, yes. Everyone knew him." That crazy act with the knives, she thought.

"What about Roger Charles?" he asked.

"Now there was an actor. A class act. Way ahead of his time. I think we may have gone out once." She eyed him closely. Of course, they had never gone out. She just wanted to see what kind of reaction she'd get.

He was right all those years to think that Roger Charles gave him class. He had his opening. With a big grin and with as much treacle as he could stuff into his gravelly voice, he said, "We're all here. Hymie, Roger, Glick. Glick Glickman at your service, M'am. How do you do?" He tipped his imaginary hat.

"How do I do *what*?" she said with a bite, keeping a straight face. No one would know she stole the line she once heard Tallulah Bankhead say in a play.

Fascinating creature, he thought.

Deciding to play a little, she said, "Glick Glickman, Glick Glickman. I'm not sure. Oh, yes, I remember. You're *that* Glick Glickman?" Game, set, match. She knew damned well he was *that* Glick Glickman.

After the few nothing tidbits they exchanged, he invited her to join him at his table. Not in the mood for conversation, she refused, but told him to ask her every day and one day she might say yes. You hussy, she thought about herself. Besides, it was Friday, and nothing was going to keep her from Happy Hour held every Friday from two to four in the afternoon in the Activities Room. It was the only time she drank. The wine was free, and it hadn't taken her long to figure out why they called it Happy Hour. To borrow a phrase… 'What happened in Happy Hour stayed in Happy Hour.'

Harry Goldberg and Oscar Shapiro were in dreamland, and that didn't mean sleeping, and would probably live forever ogling Mister and Miss Show Business. They spent their days talking about film stars, who was Jewish in Hollywood and who was not, who was dead, who was still working, who was still working *and* dead, and they quoted lines from their favorite movies, even if sometimes the lines were attributed to the wrong film and artist. It didn't matter. Somehow talking about these subjects had a way of masking their painful joints, not to mention the dental woes Oscar was now facing.

He decided not to follow the dentist's advice to go through extensive gum flaps, bone replacements, implants; whatever the procedure was called. He wasn't sure of any of the technical terms. It didn't matter since he had decided he was going to keep his teeth and gums as they were. It was his mouth, his body, and no one was going to invade any of his orifices. If he'd listened to the doctors years ago, he'd be dead by now. He already had outlived two of his physicians and one dentist, so as far as he was concerned, to hell with them all. He sought advice from Jon Sullivan who looked up 'teeth and gums' on the Internet. Oscar was advised to rinse with warm salt water three times a day, use a new Oral-B toothbrush every three months, and continue his work with the hygienist four times a year instead of only twice a year. And that was that. He could still chew serious food, oatmeal hadn't become his staple; not yet, anyway, and that's all he was concerned about.

Valeska's apartment was filled with stunning mementos of a bygone era. It was fussy, exotic, and dimly lit in a faded film star kind of way. The off-white painted walls were covered in either framed black and white stills from her films, or just of her, some in seductive poses. Some mornings she slept until noon. Other mornings she'd awaken as early as five. She never went to bed without her satin eye mask to cover her still sparkling violet eyes, a satin head scarf to cover her thinning ash blond/gray-ish white hair, satin chin mask to lift her sagging chin or chins, depending on the angle, and satin nightgown. She owned seven. They didn't make them like that anymore. She liked the luxurious feeling of satin next to her skin. In the dark, it made her feel young. In the dark, she was still in the house in Beverly Hills awaiting the arrival of her current *amoretto.*

Not wanting to be isolated and lonely, she had befriended many of the residents at West Palm Acres who were thrilled to get her attention and all agreed, she was just a regular person. She particularly liked those two crazy guys, Oscar Shapiro and Harry Goldberg. She couldn't decide if they were a couple of screaming old queens or just roommates. Not that it mattered. She had no romantic interest in either of them. Those feelings had long ago left the building, so she thought. There was someone she did like. It was more than just like. She was growing quite fond of Glick Glickman. Per her opening advice to him, every day he did ask her to join him for lunch and one day she said yes. After that, they always ate together. He had a multi-faceted personality that appealed to her. She was never bored when they were together. And she positively adored the kid, Jon Sullivan, who, to all of them, had become 'the kid.' She understood his plight totally. An actor who had to take other work in between acting jobs was no stranger to her. They often confided in one another.

Did she miss the business? Less and less. Who was she kidding? It had been wonderful. Of course she missed it. Most of all, she missed what it represented. Like that Cher person she saw giving an interview one time about aging mostly and how she hated getting old. But Valeska was finding this more or less hassle free lifestyle easier and easier to take with each passing day. Besides, she didn't care for the alternative. The saying, dead or alive, had taken on new meaning for her now. She preferred alive.

Her family rarely visited. She and her daughter had developed a sort of healthy, yet chilly phone relationship. Their rule was that Valeska would phone Anna every day when she woke up. If Anna had something important to say, she could make the first call. Valeska would get cards from her granddaughter, now happily married, but they never spoke. Valeska had hopes that one day this would change.

One morning, Valeska received a peculiar phone call from her daughter. Considering Anna's penchant for the bizarre, it wasn't that weird. The conversation, for lack of a better word, went like a vaudeville sketch.

A: Hello, Mother.

V: Who is this?

A: I'm only calling to tell you I can't call you later.

V: You're calling me now.

A: But I won't be able to call later.

V: Thanks for the message. I'll tell your mother.

A: Are you alright?

V: Now you ask.

A: I love you.

V: Love you 'til I can no longer dance on the ceiling.

A: That was not your greatest film.

V: They were all great. The writers got lousy.

A: Tomorrow, Gloria Swanson, or whoever you are today.

V: You're never alone with schizophrenia.

A: What?

V: *Caio, bella.*

Valeska wondered how she, *the* Valeska Bernhart, loved by millions, could have given birth to an alien like Anna.

It took a few seconds but then she remembered who the father was. Her second husband. The shoe salesman in the fancy boutique on Rodeo Drive in Beverly Hills. Just goes to show how you can be fooled by a handsome man in a good suit kneeling at your knees looking up your…never mind. She closed her eyes to erase the image. If she had taken as much time over marriage decisions that she took over deciding what dressing to order for her salad in a restaurant, she wouldn't have had four husbands. Oh, well, with age comes wisdom, as everyone says. Well, maybe not everyone. Where was wisdom when you needed it?

Glick Glickman had found his morning ritual. Wake up. That was number one. What else mattered? Thank you, thank you world. He enjoyed these little asides to himself. Then he would look in the bathroom mirror and say out loud, "Hello, handsome. Enjoy the image. This is the best you're going to look for the rest of your life." Good line. I gotta remember that one.

Glick's apartment resembled the eclectic inside of his former briefcase. He was never big on home décor. He had the walls painted black as a background to his colorful and numerous posters of movies and plays and movie stars. Huge colorful pillows decorated the floors. Rather than floor lamps or table lamps, Glick had arranged for lamps to be hung from the ceiling in strategic areas. A white sofa floated at an angle in the center of the living room. It always made him a little dizzy, but he never bothered to straighten it. A matching wing chair stood adjacent to the couch. His bedroom was functional without any particular style.

After Jon Sullivan finished his duties, he was often invited to have a drink with Glick in the inner sanctum. One evening over drinks of scotch and water, no ice–that is Glick drank scotch while Jon drank a glass of water from the sink since he never drank alcohol–Jon learned a valuable lesson.

He was most impressed with the way Glick kept reinventing himself through the years right up to the present. That was the way to live. Be anyone you want to be. Personally, he wasn't sure he could do that. He had to do it temporarily to play a character, but in his real life, he was who he was and told Glick, "I am what I am."

"No, it doesn't work that way," Glick said in his professorial tone. "You become who you want to be."

Jon repeated the words. In fact, they became his mantra. You become who you want to be. It gave Jon a lot of food for thought. Was he living his life the way he wanted it to be, or was he just reacting, meeting the moment? Isn't that what an actor was supposed to do? React?

Another evening, over Glick's scotch and his water, Jon asked, "Do you mind if I ask a personal question?"

"Ask. I might not answer," mused Glick.

"What really happened in New York? The Broadway thing, I mean. The papers were full of stuff but you know, kind of vague. I wasn't sure what to believe. *A Little Revue* was slated to open; then it was re-titled; then it never opened. You lost the money or you never had it or the theatre didn't want the show or you pulled out of the deal. What's the real story?"

It didn't matter anymore, so Glick decided to tell Jon what really happened, not to sound noble or a hero or anything, but because he liked the kid who was working just to make ends meet. He told him about Jane Smith turning out to be Daphne Sockafeller. "She wanted to put all the money in to back the show. At first I agreed. And then I couldn't do it. Whether it was conscience or what, I don't know. I might never know."

Jon was riveted by Glick's patterns and rhythms; the way he'd slow up, pause, speed on. He was literally speechless listening to him.

"I simply couldn't take her money. She didn't know the risks. She was just a kid. Her whole life was ahead of her. I knew she was in love with me, and I liked her, but that was all. I couldn't take the money. I couldn't be her slave. And that's what would have happened. That's when I knew it was time to hang up the toe shoes. So I cancelled everything. The worst thing was telling those four kids."

"Ruby Valk, Rocky Rage, Inky Krabb, Enzo Bordelo." Of course, Jon knew who they were, although he had never met them.

"I don't know what they're doing now. They were counting on the show, and then they were out of work again. I almost had a stroke from the whole thing. To tell you the truth, and I never thought I would ever say this, I'm glad the whole thing is over."

"What about Jane…I mean, Daphne Sockafeller?"

"We're not in touch. Listen, she was young. Still is. I'm sure she got over it and found she was very comforted by billions of dollars. Did you hear? Not millions. Billions. What can I say? And that, sir, is the story that *Variety* will never print because they will never know about it." He could have bored a hole through Jon with his look.

Jon got it. "My lips are sealed. You can trust me." Others would have raced to the newspapers or the gossip magazines and spilled the beans for money. But not Jon Sullivan.

11

ROAST BEEF

Much to the delight of the residents, Glick had become the head raconteur at West Palm Acres. Even Harry hadn't minded stepping back to become a supporting player. Now that Glick and Valeska had warmed up to one another, and now that they had accepted the fact that West Palm Acres was not a myth but the new normal with no turning back option, there was no end to the stories they shared with each other and the others about their former lives. This was more to entertain and inform rather than a 'living in the past' kind of thing.

As for Jon, all the residents had taken quite a shine to the actor in the clown suit. He had to admit he hadn't had this much fun since he played a bunch of grapes two years previous in a TV commercial for the Health Board's warning about hemorrhoids.

One evening, Glick and Valeska were sitting on the verandah in their favorite white wicker rockers. They did what people do in rockers. They rocked.

Gently.

Glick looked at her and without emotion said, "Look at this. We're in rocking chairs. And we're rocking. I suppose it could be worse. We could be sitting on a bench in Central

Park." It was something that was never going to happen to him. The rocker.

Only old folks rocked.

Valeska said, "The bench is worse than the rocker."

"Yes. All those pigeons," Glick said.

"Not to mention the cold," Valeska said.

It didn't matter. Nothing mattered. They were comfortable and rocked whenever it suited them. Suddenly they burst out laughing at themselves.

"So," she said.

"So," he said.

They both sighed.

"I've always been a little curious about something. Is Glick Glickman your real name?"

"It really is, but no one believes it. Early on, I tried to simplify it. Perry Coma. Buck Tuck. Rob Throb."

Valeska felt a routine coming on and was ready, willing, and waiting to enjoy his humor.

Glick carried on without skipping a beat. "Milton Schlumperberger. Sonny Crack. Sandy Pile. Chuck Wagon. Clark Bagle. Fidel Upjon. Jingles Jackman. Rock Bottom. Eliot Mess. Hopalong Bladder. Harold Leftover."

Valeska was laughing so hard, tears were streaming down her cheeks. She could barely get out the words, "I can see why you stuck with Glick Glickman. Or should I say Hymie Moscowitz? Or is it really Roger Charles?"

"Until I hear my name, I don't know who I am."

"Or where you are," Valeska added.

"I don't do a double act," Glick said, only half-jokingly.

That made Valeska laugh even harder. "Will the real Glick Glickman stand up?"

He stood and took a bow. Feeling a little dizzy, he immediately sat down. "What about you? Valeska Bernhart isn't exactly the girl next door."

"Real. Honest. After my great grandfather's second wife. The studio didn't change the name. I always liked it. With a name like that, I had to be destined for show business, right? Can you imagine a Valeska Bernhart turning up for the stenography pool?"

Glick laughed. "It's a good name."

"You're a funny man. You make me laugh. And that hasn't happened for a long time."

"Laughing is the new sex," he said.

"You mean like they say sixty is the new forty?"

"Or should we say, eighty is the new sixty?" he quipped.

They'd milked that one dry and moved on. Besides, it was a little too close to the bone. It was time for a new subject.

"Funny we never met," Valeska said.

"It happens. People think people in the business know everybody else in the business. We don't."

"No time when you're always working."

"Strange business," Glick said reflectively. "Only people in the business know how strange it is."

Valeska remembered thinking that same thing back in Santa Monica when she was on her way to the open casting call. "With all the disappointments, I couldn't imagine doing anything else all those years." Valeska was also in a reminiscent mood.

"Nope," Glick said. "There were the highs, too. More highs than lows, I think."

"I'm glad I did what I did when I did it."

"Yup," Glick said in his best Gary Cooper voice. "Those were the days. Nothing like it now, not that there's anything wrong with now. But they don't make them like that anymore."

"Gary Cooper, Cary Grant, Burt Lancaster," she remembered and smiled. "I knew them all. I was much much younger, of course."

"Of course you were. Rita Hayworth, Ava Gardner, Lana Turner," he sighed. "Real lookers. No one today comes close. And they didn't air brush the bodies. Those were their real bodies."

They stopped talking as they pictured the good old days. But the conversation was getting too maudlin and that wasn't them. Keep moving forward no matter what is what got each of them to where they were.

Without batting an eye, Glick slipped on his performance hat. "You wanna hear Gracie Allen's classic recipe for roast beef?" Glick was doing what he did best. He lightened up the mood.

"What?" she asked, gearing up for a routine.

"Ingredients are one large roast beef and one small roast beef."

"Why two roast beefs?" she asked, playing the straight man.

"You take the two roasts and put them in the oven. When the little one burns, the big one is done."

"Very funny, Gracie," she said. She'd enjoyed the momentary repartee with him. Just three lines and somehow, she was a performer again.

"Of course." He still had it. He would always have it. Timing.

They both sighed again.

"It's a good place," she said.

"Better than the Actors Home in Jersey," he said. "I had considered it. Glad I didn't."

"For me it was the Motion Picture and Television Country House in Woodland Hills."

"Glad you didn't. See? We both ended up here. Fate, my dear Valeska."

"Imagine that," she said. My, my, she thought. Destiny.

Thinking this might be a good moment to bring it up,

Glick broached a subject they had talked about before. "Have you thought about what we talked about?"

She knew, sooner or later, he would want her decision. "I haven't been able to think about anything else."

"And? You wanna do it?" His voice was intentionally seductive.

With a throb in her voice that gave away her doubts and slight sadness for what she was about to say, she replied, "My performing days are over. After that fiasco, that humiliation with that independent director, Tara Bombeck…I told you about it…I can't go through it anymore. It's over. I've accepted my life as it is now."

"You got paid, your name wasn't listed on the credits, so what harm was done? It ended up at obscure Film Festivals. No one even remembers or will remember. You should know some of the things I did. The jobs I did outside the business."

"Why? Why did we do it?"

"For love, doll face. That's why. For love."

"Love. There are all kinds of love."

"You still haven't given me a straight answer."

"I can't, Glick," she said, finally, but without much conviction.

He picked up on her tone. "Can't? Won't? Even you don't believe that."

"I think I do," she said sheepishly.

He wasn't giving up. "It's never over when it's in your blood. We just did a spontaneous routine together. Nothing profound. It was about roast beef. We fit like a glove on a hand. And it was fun. For those few seconds, we weren't Valeska and Glick. Well, we were, but in other people's shoes."

"I don't think I would have the energy." Did she just need a good reason?

"You won't be out there alone. I'll be with you."

And there was the reason.

12

THE COMEBACK

With the announcement that Valeska Bernhart and Glick Glickman would be returning to the stage, the buzz in the community had been high. And now the day had come. The residents gathered in the West Palm Acres Theatre anticipating a real treat. Trussed up like turkeys at Thanksgiving, Oscar Shapiro and Harry Goldberg stood out among the casually dressed folks. To Oscar and Harry, this was an opening night on Broadway even though it was three o'clock on a Tuesday afternoon. Respect must be paid to actors; therefore, you didn't show up to a performance in shorts and sneakers.

Two chaise lounges had been pre-set on stage by Jon Sullivan who had been cast as the stage manager and announcer. For this type of event, he was allowed to remove his clown suit. He looked quite normal, almost handsome, in regular trousers and a shirt.

Jon announced, "Written and directed by Glick Glickman, the brief skit is about two senior citizens who have moved in with their children who happen to be married to each other. Our very own Valeska Bernhart plays Dora and our Glick Glickman plays Murray. Dora is the mother of the wife and Murray is the father of the husband. The setting is the pool at their home in Beverly Hills. You will have to imagine the pool," he chuckled, hoping to warm up the audience.

Costumed in matching light blue and white velour warm-up suits which they purchased at a local Target, Valeska and Glick entered to healthy applause. Valeska had been convinced by Glick to lose the cane for the performance. She protested, but eventually gave in. It was a prop, yes, but not one she needed on stage. The applause died down, and the actors began.

In character, Glick and Valeska bend down in an attempt to touch their toes.

There is much laughter from the audience. One of the residents seated in the third row shouts, "Good luck with that!" He gets a few understanding snickers. The actors are professional enough to ignore the disruption and sail into the dialogue.

GLICK: 7...12...40...65...84...95...98...100. Okay, done.

Some laughter from the audience as the actors, out of breath, collapsed onto the chaise lounges.

VALESKA: After supper, we can run into Westwood Village. It's playing there.

GLICK: Save yourself the trouble. I'm telling you, Woody Allen never says, 'Play it again, Sam.' He says, 'Play it, Sam.'

VALESKA: I'm not talking about Woody Allen. I'm talking about the earlier movie with Ingrid Bergman.

GLICK: Casablanca.

VALESKA: That's the one.

GLICK: I don't think so.

VALESKA: I know so.

GLICK: I'll get my son, the doctor, to call what's-her-name to check it out. She's a patient.

VALESKA: How would she remember? She's made a million movies since then. Besides, she can't be a patient. She's been dead a thousand years.

GLICK: So at least she could tell us who to call who would know.

Figuring the line would get a laugh, he had directed Valeska to stretch out her arms and circle her wrists, which she did. Glick copied the gesture. With this bit of business, they kept up the action during the laugh. He knew his stuff.

The line got a laugh and scattered applause. They eased off with the hand exercise.

GLICK: Okay, smarty pants. Who is this? Over seventy-five, looks sixty, made fifty-eight films, entertained troops in three wars, belongs to eighteen golf clubs, possesses over two thousand trophies including a congressional medal from President Kennedy, has Eddie Foy's dancing shoes, has been on a first-name basis with eight presidents, and is still working. Who is it?

Someone shouted out from the audience, "A workaholic!"

Being the professionals they were, Valeska and Glick ignored the crack.

GLICK: Guess. World famous. Lives around here.

VALESKA: I give up.

GLICK: Bob Hope.

VALESKA: Bob Hope? He's dead. Why didn't you say that? You have to say it in the past tense.

GLICK: It's funnier this way.

VALESKA: Always a comedian. Bob Hope should have had you as his writer.

GLICK: I was too busy.

VALESKA: Everyone I know is dead.

The laugh they thought would come on that line didn't happen. She continued.

VALESKA: Okay, I got one for you. Famous, handsome, rich.

GLICK: Brad Pitt.

Unable to control himself, Harry Goldberg shouted out, "George Clooney." Oscar Shapiro elbowed him in the ribs to keep still.

Attention spans ran short on the reservation. The natives were getting restless. Glick knew it was time to bring the skit to a close. Glick made a sound like a snore. She knew it meant to wind this up and cut to the Sleeping Beauty dialogue for the finale.

GLICK: Yesterday, I ate one hundred and thirty-two prunes in one minute and fourteen seconds. Today...today... Excuse me.

He ran off stage. The audience gasped, some really believing he was ill.

VALESKA: Now that's tsuris.

Glick returned to applause and laughter from the audience, led by Goldberg and Shapiro, and someone telling everyone to be quiet because it wasn't over.

GLICK: I heard Sleeping Beauty had halitosis.

VALESKA: Prince Charming didn't have a nose.

GLICK: Now that's mahzel.

VALESKA: Poor Sleeping Beauty. Asleep for a hundred years in all that filth. Prince Charming finally shows up, and he turns out to be a queen.

The actors stopped talking and took their bows to laughter and much applause and shouts of "encore, encore." However, it could have been, "enough, enough," so Glick knew to bring it to a close. Keep them wanting more was his motto. He was ecstatic. He was back. He was definitely back. He only hoped Valeska felt the same way he did.

The entertainment ended with Jon doing his juggling act with oranges. His timing was off. Not with the fruit. That he could do. He wasn't exactly a main attraction because everyone was more interested in the tea, lemonade, and cookies that two members of the staff were wheeling down the aisles on a cart.

Oscar and Harry congratulated their friends on a marvelous performance and joined the other residents over refreshments to brag about their personal relationship with the stars. After a brief mingle with the residents, Glick accompanied Valeska back to her apartment. They lingered outside her door. It was rare she ever entertained in her apartment, but this was a special occasion. She hadn't yet come down from the heady experience of performing, and it would be nice not to be alone. He accepted her invitation to join her.

She wasn't quite sure how she felt. She liked the applause. She knew it was a joy working with Glick. That much she knew. He had a charismatic quality, and she was drawn to him like a magnet on a fridge. But she had to be careful. She mustn't be guilty of not listening to her own belief system. In this business, people fell in love with the characters played, not the person. They were just crushes on the talent. It took a long time for her to figure it out. That's what she had told Tara Bombeck. She had to remember that now. She couldn't afford to get her heart involved; not at this stage of her life.

"Well?" he asked, sitting on the couch. "What do you think?"

"About the act?" she asked.

"Of course about the act. What do you think I'm talking about?"

She was just checking. "It went well." She sat down next to him.

"Well? Well? That's all you can say? Valeska, we were dynamite."

She cocked her head slightly and thought about it. "Yes. Yes, we were."

"You're terrific by yourself; I'm terrific by myself; but together we are great. We can still do it. Listen, I got a plan." He stood up and started to pace around the room. "We can live here or we can get a big apartment together. Maybe a bungalow. We can get a manager. No, forget that. I'll manage us. We'll play colleges, churches, retirement joints, regional theatres. There's no end to the possibilities." He sat down again. "It ain't over 'til it's over."

He'd said she was terrific. She never thought she'd hear those words again. But she had to be careful. Did she want to do it again? And did he know what he was saying? It was just the adrenalin rushing through his veins after being in front of an audience. "I'm tired, Glick."

"So am I. So we'll be a little more tired. When we're dead, we'll have plenty of time to rest."

"I like it here, Glick, at West Palm Acres. I didn't think I would, but I do. It's safe. In a short time, I have become comfortable. I don't want to stir it all up again. I don't want to travel." She wanted to be sure he heard her. "I like the status-quo. It's a peace I never really knew. Not for a long time. Can you understand that?"

"I understand. No I don't. He proposes; she refuses. He says yes; she says no. It reminds me of that old Sadie joke. Remember?"

She smiled. "I haven't heard that one in a thousand years."

Within a second, he was into the routine. With a Yiddish accent, Glick threw out the first line. "Sadie, darling, take off your nightgown."

Valeska was right with him in character. "No."

"Take off your nightgown."

"Go away."

"Sadie, please."

"Myron, please."

"Don't you want to fool around?"

"I'm hiding in the closet."

"Sadie, I'm gonna break down that closet door. One… two…"

"All of a sudden you're Mister Superman. You can't even take off my nightgown, how you gonna break down a door?"

They came out of character laughing. "See? We're good together," Glick said.

"Before, you used the word great." Valeska was laughing so hard, tears were streaming down her cheeks. "You always make my eyes water."

"Because I'm funny and because you love it."

She nodded in agreement. He was right. How could she dispute it? She wiped her eyes.

After a brief pause, he said in a mellow tone, "Do you miss it?"

"I just told you."

"No. Not that. You know. It."

She knew what 'it' meant. The conversation had done a three hundred and sixty degree turn. They'd never talked in an intimate way before. This was another side of Glick. She was amazed that she didn't mind. She had nothing to lose by being honest. She'd never told anyone how she felt about this particular subject.

"I miss it. Not all the time. Some of the time. But it's easier for a woman. Before a certain age, the law protects her. After a certain age, nature takes care of her."

"That's a funny line," he said.

"It's true," she said.

They were getting closer. Shared inner thoughts will do that. "Don't you want to fool around?" Glick said, mimicking the Myron character in the Sadie joke.

"Glick, come on, I'm too old for you." Did she really mean that? Her heart. Her heart. She could still be vulnerable, even at her age. She had to protect her heart.

"What's that got to do with it?" He made a quick decision. He stood up and with a great flourish, he ripped off his toupee and tossed it onto a chair. "Not that much older."

His flamboyant gesture took her by surprise. "You're kidding," she said, looking at his bald dome. "Wow!" His bushy eyebrows absolutely popped out at you without the top hair to balance. "I mean, wow, look at how handsome you are." She didn't want it to be obvious that she was trying to glimpse behind his ears; but there was the evidence. The scars. He'd had work done, the old son of a gun. She wished she hadn't said the 'wow.' Who knows what message it sent him?

"This is the real me, kiddo. Off-stage, sans make-up and all that camouflage, this is me now." There wasn't anybody who saw him so bare, not even Jane Daphne Smith Sockafeller.

"What the hell." With gusto, Valeska stood and removed her black wig and tossed it onto the chair where it overlapped with Glick's hairpiece. Out in the open now, her thinning wisps of gray hair were free from bondage. There were no scars behind her ears because she had never had any work done. This thought came to her only because she was sure Glick was taking a sneak peek.

Naked above the neck, they had both bared their souls. How more intimate could anyone get? They stared at one another without uttering a word, even though jaws dropped slightly and lips parted a tiny bit as if to speak; but then thinking better, each remained silent. The saying, 'Actions speak louder than words' was never truer than at this moment. Words were not necessary to express that they preferred themselves *avec* hair. And besides, the moment had passed. They'd had enough truth. Slowly, she went over to the chair, picked up her wig and placed it back on her head. Not wanting to seem too concerned about the whole incident, she chose not to look in the mirror hanging on the wall. Giving the thing a few pats, she hoped it was on straight. He took the cue and put his hairpiece back on. Vanity ruled. He didn't even want to be buried without his toupee. He made a mental note to add that point in his will.

What Glick said next was very profound. "You know, Valeska, who we see in the mirror and who we really are in life are two different images."

"Is that another one of your famous Glickmanisms?" she asked, coyly. What they had just been through was the most connected she'd been with someone of the opposite sex in years; maybe ever.

"Got it inside a Chinese fortune cookie," Glick said, dismissing the whole notion.

Valeska didn't know whether to believe him or not. It didn't matter. She felt the way she felt and that cookie wasn't going to crumble and spoil her fantasy.

"Change of topic," Glick said. "So what will it be? We'll do a show now and again? Yes?"

"Where?" She wasn't going to put herself out in the world again to be eaten alive. She knew where it had to be, but she wanted to hear it from him.

"Where else? The West Palm Acres Theatre will do nicely. It's what you want. If it was good enough for Steve and Eydie, it's good enough for us. What else can I say?" Glick had surrendered to the woman's charms. It would be the West Palm Acres Theatre, even if he secretly dreamed of playing the Kravis Center for the Performing Arts. He didn't quite realize how far he had come on his personal life journey.

That's what she wanted to hear. "It will do nicely." She was tingling all over.

They sat next to each other on the sofa looking at one another. Just looking. There wasn't any need to verbalize it. They both knew they were entering a new chapter.

"In the movies, this is where they cut to a train passing through a tunnel," he said, reaching for her hand.

"Trains, tunnels, fireworks," she said. "I know. Some type of an explosion."

They sat for a while longer without speaking. They were thinking about trains, tunnels, and fireworks, much too tired to do anything about it. It didn't matter. Tomorrow was another day.

13

JON'S EPIPHANY

Jon got that long awaited call from his agent to come back to New York for a job. Once the call came, there was no hesitating. He knew what he had to do. He was an actor. He had to go back. It was a TV commercial about black pepper. He'd worked for the advertising firm before and didn't have to audition. They wanted 'the redhead.' No other actor would do. It would be a lucrative job, and Jon always needed money. The prospect of working again in his profession excited him. Okay, so it wasn't Broadway or a movie; it was a commercial for TV, but still, he had to play a character, so that was still acting. It was no longer a stigma in the profession to do commercials. He took a leave of absence from West Palm Acres, said goodbye to his friends who were sorry to see him go but happy for his good fortune. Once he got back to New York and his milieu, he was sure he wouldn't want to return to Florida, but didn't have the heart to tell anyone.

He flew home, picked up the ad copy from his agent's office and studied it. He absolutely hated it. In fact, he was thinking up excuses to get out of it. But it was like dope in front of a user, which he never had been. But when he weighed up the positives, he was an addict. It would mean exposure in a very public medium. It might lead to a shot in a Broadway show. A television series. He was an actor. He had to do it. He memorized the words, which as it turned out wasn't even necessary, since he was to do it as a voice over. Animation was going to be used with some kind of stick figures. His agent failed to tell him that little vital fact. It turned out it had been a last minute decision and even his agent didn't know, according to his agent. Crazy, crazy, crazy. So why did they need his red hair if he wasn't even going to be seen? What a waste of time. He could have phoned it in. Still, it was good to keep the brain honed. An actor needs two things to keep the machine oiled: memory and money.

Jon sailed through it in one take using his voice's lower register and was thanked for his speedy work. It was good money, but the problem was he never felt so empty in all his life. Is this what he wanted to do for the rest of his life? He hadn't felt this depressed in months. It was a fitful sleep that night during which it came to him in an epiphany what his life's work was meant to be. It wasn't to wait around so see if someone else thought he was good enough to play a role. It certainly wasn't to look forward to a future of playing a bunch of purple grapes or selling black pepper. He didn't want to return to what he now saw as the nothingness in New York. Let the other actors kill themselves out there. The ridiculousness of this last job finished it for him. He knew what he wanted to do, even if at the moment, he didn't know how he was going to do it. He couldn't wait to return to West Palm Acres.

14

THE BENEFITS OF CREATIVITY

Jon wanted to have a Festival of Arts for the elderly to showcase their painting, crafts, writing, music, acting abilities. He didn't think it was a new concept, but it had never been done at this location. He visualized exhibits, concerts, demonstrations, and workshops. There was more to the elders than shuffling from their apartments to the dining room, to doctors' appointments, and back home again to plunk down in front of the television or sit on a rocker on the front porch. Jon told Glick about his idea. Glick was very interested and the wheels started to turn.

"It's such a good idea, kid, I wish I'd thought of it. The title will be important. It's gotta be a grabber."

"Senior Arts Festival," said Jon. "What else can it be?"

Glick was against it. "Put seniors or elders in the title, and you're dead before you begin. No one will come to see a bunch of *alter kockers* wearing a smock and dragging around an easel and an acrylic paintbrush, doing cartwheels on the lawn, tap dancing on the ceiling, or reading poetry they've written."

"So what do we call it? How will people know what it is?" asked Jon.

They kicked around a few titles. Nothing sounded right.

And then, "I got it." Glick wrote something on a piece of paper and handed it to Jon. "It's better if you see it written down."

Jon took the piece of paper and read the words, "Second Spring Festival of the Arts." It was right. He knew it. "Second Spring. I love it."

Glick repeated the name. As he said it, he knew that was it. It had class. It said what it was and there was no senior or elder in the title. "Wait. I got a better one. Listen to this. Spring Again. What do you think?"

Jon repeated, "Second Spring." He paused, then, "Spring Again." He paused. "I think I like that one better. Spring Again: Festival of the Arts. No. Second Spring Festival of the Arts."

"We can always change the title," Glick said. That's how creativity worked. You never had to get anchored to one thing.

So now that they had the concept, all that was needed was the doing of it. Glick was sure the money could be found among large corporations, foundations, federal grants, as well as from generous donors and patrons of the arts. This was good clean fun, not what he had to go through in New York with the Fat Cats of the world. He hadn't lost his gift of the gab. He'd make it happen.

Jon was bubbling over with excitement as he laid out his idea for Glick. He hadn't felt this exhilarated about a project in years. It would begin right there in West Palm Beach, but maybe it would extend to other cities. A whole weekend event. But that was later. It wouldn't just be residents at West Palm Acres. What about all those people who lived independently in the area and were still creating? The process in itself of putting on such an event would be creative. It wouldn't be difficult to reach people through the Internet. Everybody had computers these days. From a four year old to a ninety year old, they knew how to tap those keys. He was pretty sure he could figure out how to get this going. Just because he had never done anything like it didn't mean he couldn't do it. And besides, Glick Glickman had taken on the role of his mentor, so he couldn't possibly fail.

Glick cautioned against Jon's idea for a weekend event. "It's good to think big, but let's start with one day. You'll have to put together a proposal of your idea and take it to management here. That's the third step. The first was coming up with the idea; the second was talking it out with me. You see how these things build?"

Jon read up on the aging process. There were endless reports on the subject. Research had shown how beneficial creativity was for older folks. Tremendous benefits were to be gained. For a start, they lived longer. Creativity relieved stress, lowered blood pressure and cholesterol levels. Without outside distractions like making a living, the mind was free to soar. Without the worry of the upkeep of a house, yard work, and bill paying, they were free to enjoy the fruits of their hard-earned labor. It was known that expressive writing had serious health benefits, not just for the aged but for people of any age who expressed themselves on paper. Fewer stress-related visits to the doctor, improved immune system functioning, improved lung function, reduced blood pressure, fewer days in hospital, improved moods, a feeling of greater psychological well-being, improved memory.

In his off hours, because he was still the medical clown, Jon put together a proposal and went to the management at West Palm Acres with the plan. It didn't take much to convince them. They were overwhelmed with enthusiasm. A committee had to be formed to drive it. Glick and Valeska were the first to sign up followed by the executive director of the Chamber of Commerce and two other leaders in the West Palm Beach community. The committee laid the plans to approach participants in the immediate area and even a bit beyond. It was hoped these folks would agree to showcase their talent and be part of such an undertaking.

With something as small as an announcement in the monthly Retirement Guide Magazine that people picked up for free in grocery stores, money, ideas, and support were forthcoming. People knew what the expression 'second spring' meant without hammering it home to them. The results were exquisite. Many many people wanted to participate. Just to name a few, there was Elena Faust who started dance lessons in 1922 at age three and, at ninety-two, continued teaching in Palm Beach, seated erect in a chair, gesturing elegantly with her arms. She was on board along with Shirley Wasserman. At eighty-five, Wasserman had just published a memoir about her life in South Africa and India in the days when no one did it. And there was Joseph Regis who at eighty-four was still teaching the art of black and white film at the University of Miami. He put the committee onto Edna King who began sculpting at the age of sixty-nine and now at age seventy-nine was having one woman shows around the world. And that was just the beginning. These were some of the known people. Jon wanted to showcase the unsung heroes. As the committee worked on the project, they uncovered all the talent in the immediate area. They doubted it could be held as a one day event. However, it was agreed it could be a mistake to be overly ambitious too soon.

And so, the beginning of Jon Sullivan's new life was underway. He found a replacement for himself as pseudo-medical clown. He got out of his apartment and commitments in New York. His agent wasn't too disappointed. It would be one less hopeful whose heart he didn't have to break for lack of work. Jon found a modest one-bedroom apartment in West Palm Beach close to West Palm Acres and, for the first time since moving away from the family home, he was able to tell his parents what he really did.

Glick was on a roll. He went to meetings, he wrote, he directed. His mind was as sharp as a Gillette razor. Overloaded with confidence, in his old style of a combination of *chutzpah* and an ability to communicate verbally, he convinced the city to donate space for the event at the Convention Center downtown. Monetary support for advertising the event was flying in from patrons of the arts. Volunteers were on hand to set it up. Glick had a slight battle with some of the supporters about the name. The money people thought that the word 'seniors' or 'elders' had to be in the title. How else will people know what it is? Glick stuck to his guns and said it would turn people away, both young and old; that it could serve as an example for young people to show them what was ahead; that it didn't have to be pills and the couch in front of the television. In the end, he won out and his title remained. That is, they were back to the original: Second Spring. It turned out that Spring Again was actually being used by a similar group in Wisconsin or Kansas. Somewhere out that way.

Glick wrote a comic monologue for Valeska. He outlined it for her. "The character has to make a decision whether or not to marry her fiancé and goes through the pros and cons until a decision is made," he explained. "Simple, but deep."

At first, she balked, saying it was too difficult, that it wasn't believable, and that she was too old for that scenario. Glick told her she was not looking at the glass half-full; but rather, she was seeing it half-empty. He knew the problem. She was scared. He convinced her she was ageless. And besides, isn't she the actress who could play characters twenty years her junior and get away with it? Wasn't it Van Gogh who said there was no such thing as an old woman? Glick knew how to get what he wanted because it didn't take long before she agreed to do it. Rehearsals began. He directed every line, every nuance, and she took direction well. It felt grand to be doing it again. For both of them. Beyond grand. But it wasn't 'again.' It was new and best of all, it was now.

15

SECOND SPRING FESTIVAL OF THE ARTS

It had taken five months and fifteen days of concentrated organizing and planning, but the day had finally arrived. Artists, musicians, writers, actors, actresses, and dancers from ages seventy to over one hundred gathered together to display their talent. The eldest, at one hundred and two, Josephine Stem, wanted the naysayers to know she didn't begin writing her memoir until she was ninety-five. She wrote her stories out longhand and her granddaughter got it into the computer. What a wonderful celebration and gift to her family. Mary Sheppard wanted everyone to know that at the age of ninety-six, she was working on the third book of her trilogy about the Civil War. She said in an interview that the determination to write is like having a benign but chronic disease. It can sometimes go into remission, but can never be cured.

With the publicity and marketing saying that *the* Valeska Bernhart would be performing, people flocked to the Festival. The whole thing was enhanced by the fact that the November-timed event captured the snowbirds who had begun to arrive. Valeska was to appear as the finale, thereby guaranteeing the audience would stay. A special dressing room had been set up backstage for her. And surprise of all surprises, her daughter, son-in-law, granddaughter, and her husband all came. Glick never wanted Valeska to know that he had been the one to arrange it.

In her dressing room, Glick told her how lovely she looked. She had donned an old, but fabulous, lavender dress that still fit and brought out the magnificent color of her eyes. For the occasion, she replaced the black wig with a handsome platinum blonde wig convinced it made her look younger. It did. It wasn't Veronica Lake or Marilyn Monroe; still, very attractive. Upon reflection, it wasn't anybody except Valeska Bernhart.

"I can see it all now," Valeska was orating. "A tiny blurb in *Entertainment Weekly* following Births, Splits, and the Ailing under the Deaths column: Golden Age star passes at 95."

"It's just nerves, my dear. Just nerves. The old butterflies are getting into the act."

"What's it been for?"

"For all of it, kiddo. For the before, the during, and the after. For the now."

"Oh, shut-up, Glick."

"Ninety-five is too young. Why not a hundred and five?"

"You're crazy."

"Crazy is my middle name." He studied her. "Scared?"

"A little. No. Yes. I was. Not now."

"That's my girl. By the way, Betty Grable didn't have anything on those pins of yours."

"Lloyds of London insured her legs for a million bucks."

"That's because they hadn't seen yours."

Risking it, she had slipped into a pair of three inch heels which after days and days of sneakers felt like fifteen inches. Those legs had been her trademark and she had every intention of displaying them. Once again, she discarded her cane for the performance.

"Get out there now and show `em how it's done." He kissed her on the cheek.

She only hoped she wouldn't break her neck in the dangerously high heeled shoes. Anyway, she wasn't worried about it. If she fell, Glick would be there to catch her.

Valeska waited in the wings as Glick made the introduction. She took three deep breaths and was as ready as she would ever be. She said her usual prayer before a performance: "Please God, don't let me make a fool of myself."

She entered majestically to a totally unexpected standing ovation. People remembered Valeska Bernhart. No longer the fading film star, the invisible has-been, she was alive and kicking. It felt as if she'd never been away. She recovered quickly from the adulation. She had to. She was about to perform. The audience settled down. She was in character and ready to say the words that had been written just for her. After a slight pause…that crucial pause just before you begin intended to keep the audience in a state of expectation…she took a deep breath and began her lines.

"I'm getting married." Brief pause. Timing was everything in a piece like this. "I'm marrying Jerome Kanter. Jerome and I met through mutual friends at a dinner party. We talked and talked and talked. I lied. He lied. It was a perfect match." Another beat.

That brought the first laugh from the audience. She knew how long to wait before going on. She knew when to continue with a slightly raised voice so there wouldn't be total silence before the laughter died out. It was just a thin hair of a moment. And she knew how to do it. She knew, too, when *not* to pause, when *not* to take a breath. It was all about that one word: timing.

"Jerome is six feet tall and I'm five feet tall, but when we're in bed together we're the same height. What I'm wondering is where do the extra inches go?"

Laughter from the audience, accompanied by a smattering of applause, gave her what she wanted. It was a funny line made even funnier by her delivery.

"When Jerome and I got engaged, he gave me a ring. It was cubic zirconia from the Home Shopping Network."

This got a huge laugh.

"To celebrate, he bought tickets to a foreign film. He couldn't get two seats together on the same night. I went Thursday and he went Friday. He flew to Paris. His telegram read: 'Feeling new man. Staying extra week.' My telegram read, 'So am I. Stay as long as you like.'"

Raucous laughter was accompanied by applause. She was smoking hot. Out of the corner of her eye, she could see Glick standing in the wings. He blew her a kiss. You never know how what you write is going to be received. He had just gone with his instinct. It was paying off. Valeska was brilliant. And just as an aside, she was ageless out there. Love can do that to you. All kinds of love. He ran a hand down the back of his head just to check his hair was on securely. This would not be a good time for any mishaps.

Valeska continued, "When Jerome came back, I made a special cheesecake for him."

As if it hadn't been rehearsed, Jon Sullivan had been directed to shout out from the audience, "What's so special about cheesecake?"

In character, Valeska shouted back to the planted heckler, "I make it without cheese."

It didn't get a laugh. It hadn't worked. People were taking too long to figure out how to make cheesecake without cheese. Maybe tofu? But then it would be called tofu cheesecake. Glick made a mental note to change the line for any future performances. Maybe cut it completely.

"I'm having lots of doubts about this marriage. I hate to

cook and when we get married, I'll be responsible for his entire digestive tract."

"Eat out," another planted heckler shouted. This brought a spattering of laughter, but mostly cries of "be quiet" and "ssh."

All in one breath, Valeska delivered a whopper. "When we get married I'll have to give up Max and Lou and Archie and Wendell and Oscar and Harry."

Her delivery was spot on because the auditorium erupted with shrieks and howls of laughter. Glick had been clever enough to use the names of real men at West Palm Acres. Recognition is what made it so funny.

When Valeska was able to be heard, she said with resignation, "I've always been the other woman. If I'm the wife, will there be another woman? Can I be both the wife and the other woman?" She sighed. "I don't think I'm ready."

"Pick me," a man called out. He hadn't been planted. It got a laugh.

Valeska continued, "This is an important step. I take more time deciding what shoes to wear."

Another laugh from the spectators, especially the women.

"There is only one prerequisite for divorce. Marriage."

The laugh was there, but now the audience was with her in a different kind of way; more involved in her plight; waiting for her decision.

"If it works for unmarried people to live together, would it work for married people to live apart?"

The audience was silent, but they were thinking.

"There are a lot worse things than marriage." She took a beat to think about it. "Like falling off a cliff and breaking a hip." Raising her voice, she said, "Or a lukewarm martini with a hair in it."

That was the key line. The audience burst into laughter and broke into applause. It gave her a chance to mentally and physically take a rest. Not so much that it affected her character; but just enough time for the actress to take a breath and rejuvenate. Just a little trick never noticed by an audience; the moment to make a transition from one line to another.

"We might go down in history with all the great lovers: Antony and Cleopatra. Romeo and Juliet. Doris Day and Rock Hudson. Jack Klugman and Tony Randall."

"Lillie Scott and Clark Acton," shouted out a prune-faced West Palm Acres female resident, definitely not a plant. Lillie and Clark were fuming and a little embarrassed as if they had no idea everyone knew about their nightly romps down the hallway on the third floor of building C.

Laughter was accompanied by a lot of reprimands for the gossipmonger to be quiet.

Valeska couldn't resist Madeline Kahn's line from *Blazing Saddles* which she sent out to the heckler. "Are you in show business? No? Then get the hell off my stage." She put her hands on her hips and glared at the heckler. "I don't do a double act, sister." The applause told her she had reacted appropriately. She looked over at Glick who gave her a thumbs up.

She continued. "Electric ovens, waffle irons, washing machines, dirty shirts, dirty socks, dirty sheets. No longer my bed. Our bed. Oh, goodie, I love a crowd."

Anticipating a laugh here, she paused. Maybe they hadn't heard because there was no laugh. She covered the pause by placing her voice higher for the beginning of the next bit. Sailing in without a break in the dialogue, she said, "Marriage is happiness. What's happy? One of the seven dwarfs. Jerome laughs a lot. I like to wake up in the morning with a smile on my face. Maybe I should sleep with a hanger in my mouth. Jerome wears dark blue suits. He smokes cigars. So do I. He snores. So do I. Marriage is security. Security is flying in an airplane. You know beforehand all the terrible things that can happen. What marriage offers that kind of guarantee?"

And that's when she stopped talking the way Glick had directed her. He said she would get a big laugh at the end if she did it that way. And he was right. The audience held it in as long as they could, and as if they had been trapped in a pressure cooker, they exploded. It was nearly a full sixty seconds—a long time on stage—before the audience settled down.

She continued. "Should I? Shouldn't I? Should I? Shouldn't I? Jerome is intelligent, kind, handsome, rich, and good." In a Mae West imitation, she repeated the last words with a different meaning. "And good."

A few chuckles from an attentive audience. They were waiting for her decision about whether or not to marry Jerome.

"I like Jerome. I don't love him. He loves me. He doesn't like me. And there's my answer. Missus. Not as good as Miss," she said, using full resonance. Valeska shook her head up and down. She had figured it out.

The audience was one hundred percent with her as they sensed the climax was coming. You could hear a pin drop.

And then Valeska delivered the punch line the way a punch line was meant to be delivered...with punch. "The most fascinating thing about Jerome is...me."

She held a couple of seconds, took one step back, and bowed. It was over. The audience applauded and one by one stood to pay homage. Respect was being paid to an oldie but a goodie; to someone who had endured and sustained. It was the name of the game. Valeska was flushed with pride. She was being honored. The suffering, the ups and downs, the times in between the jobs, the good times, the bad times... it hadn't been a waste. She was seven years old at her first ever performance doing a recitation in front of the school assembly in Brooklyn. But this was better.

During the standing ovation, Glick rushed on stage and embraced her. It was evident the audience was clamoring for more. He suggested in a whisper to her that as an encore they do the Sadie joke and then get off. She nodded approval. They hadn't rehearsed it, but they knew what to do. It was a sensational send-off to the entire Festival.

Later backstage, a local reporter and a photographer were in their faces with a camera and a notebook. Glick refused to be interviewed without Jon whose brainchild it had all been. Jon was located and the usual questions began with the trio being most cooperative.

"What's the secret to staying active and creative? Is it a gift? Can anyone have it?" asked the newsman.

Glick bellowed, "Love life. Not meaning one's love life. That's okay, too. But I mean, you have to love life."

Valeska added, "It's a gift to be alive."

Jon's two words summed it up. "Stay curious."

Glick held up his hand as a signal the interview was over. He knew how to leave them wanting more and he knew a good curtain line when he heard it.

The Festival had been a success. It was decided to do one every other year. It had done what Jon Sullivan intended it to do. This was just the beginning. It wasn't too early to begin planning. No one said it, but who knew how long anyone would be around? It was the process that would keep them going. It reminded Jon of an ancient Japanese poem he'd once seen at an art exhibit in New York. *I know not where my love will go; only the meeting is everything.* He thought it could be applied in this situation. Television cameras, reporters, all kinds of news junkies swarmed around. Who said you can only be in the spotlight as an actor? He was more visible now than he had ever been. Not that that was his goal. What he liked about it was he was giving, not taking. God worked in the most mysterious ways. He'd found his niche. All he had had to do was reinvent himself by taking off the old like you would shed a coat.

Maybe Glick's revival didn't take place on Broadway. "Broadway, Schmoadway," he told Valeska and Jon. "I got a script, I got an actress, I got a stage. A revival is a revival."

Jon had underscored the point that research had already proved. Simply stated, creativity was the key. It was a way to age without getting older. He had come down to Florida for what he thought would be a couple of months in between acting jobs. Instead, he couldn't imagine living anywhere else. It had turned out to be quite a gig. He had given up acting and, in his opinion, was really creating now. With Jon at the helm, the seed committee members planned to meet regularly to layout the arrangements for the next Festival.

16

OFF-STAGE

The two *second springers* had found one other, not as the people they had been in the past, but as they were today. Glick Glickman, former showman, entrepreneur, director, writer, so on and so forth; and Valeska Bernhart, former film and stage star. Glick was still a writer/director. Valeska was still an actress. But each had grown a new skin. They had that spontaneous reaction that individuals have towards each other; that mutual sense of attraction and understanding. Not only were they compatible in a professional sense, having been restored to who they once were in a new refreshed way, but their personal lives had taken on new meaning. Romance had blossomed. And chemistry is chemistry. The heart wants what the heart wants. Who's to say what the right kind of love is? Or when it should be? Love lives longer than time, whatever that means. Sometimes love comes early, but it can come later, too. Who's to say when it is better or right? It comes when it comes. It comes when needed. It can happen anywhere to anyone. If it's meant. Whatever that means.

The two of them were in her apartment relaxing and gabbing over a cup of coffee. It seemed they could always find something to talk about. She was in a playful mood.

"Wait until you see this." Just for fun, she pulled a cardboard box out from her hall closet.

"I sense a show coming on." He clapped his hands. "I love a good show." He got comfortable and waited.

One by one, Valeska pulled out hats from the carton. "They don't make them like these anymore. You'd have to get them handcrafted." She put an enormous yellow straw hat on her head and checked herself in the small mirror hanging on the wall. Artificial pink, red, and purple flowers dripped from the rim. She pulled the sheer pink veil down to cover her face. "I wore this one year in the Burbank Easter parade." She posed, sucking in her cheeks. "I was a sensation."

Glick was beaming when he said, "I bet you were."

Next, Valeska donned a cloche. The close-fitting jade green hat with no brim framed her face beautifully. "The studio let me keep this after I played in that film about speakeasies in Chicago. You know, I can't even remember the name." She batted her eyelids at Glick.

"It suits you," Glick said, putting his palms together and making the motion of clapping.

Valeska rummaged around in the box. "Oh, no, I haven't thought about this in years." She pulled out a shiny trumpet and held it with both her hands. "Do I dare?" She held it up and looked at it as if she were greeting an old friend.

"Dare," he said, egging her on. "Dare."

"Should I, shouldn't I?" she said, quoting a line from her monologue. She wiped off the mouthpiece. "I may be rusty."

With great anticipation, he swept out his hand using a gesture that indicated he was giving her the floor. "Hit it," he said.

"Okay, here goes. Oh. Any requests? I hope you say *Two Sleepy People*. It's the only number I know. Maybe."

Glick called out, "*Two Sleepy People*."

"You got it, sir." Valeska lifted the instrument to her lips, puffed out her cheeks, and blew into the mouthpiece. To her amazement, it did sound like the tune. It wasn't great but neither was it horrible.

"Bravo," Glick said, applauding. He stood up and gave her a hug.

Valeska's cheeks were flushed, the way they always did after a performance. Her eyes were sparkling as she looked at Glick. She never thought it would happen again. She didn't mean the trumpet. As far as the brass, she might pass on that in the future. She meant something else. She meant more. Much more.

17

FIREWORKS AND THE OCEAN

They became inseparable. To their surprise, they took up jogging. Suffice it to say, it was *their* version of the upwardly mobile run. Really more of a fast shuffle. It didn't matter. No one was looking. They were moving. That was the point. They watched a lot of movies. He still drove, so occasionally they went off the plantation as Glick liked to sometimes call West Palm Acres. It might be to a nearby restaurant or to window shop in Palm Beach.

But their favorite thing to do next to performing was to drive the short distance to the beach and watch the blue waves washing up on the shore. The sight of the ocean had both a calming and an energizing effect on them.

It was a gloriously mild day. They were sitting on two deck chairs looking out at the waves gently skimming the shore. Up and back. In and out.

"It's turned out to be a nice gig, hasn't it, Miss Bernhart?" he asked. He wasn't referring to the material he wrote for them or to the hours they spent rehearsing in case they were asked to perform.

She knew exactly what he meant. "Very pleasant, indeed, Mr. Glickman," she said, adding, "And still going."

"*Viva la gig,*" he said and sighed again.

"*Viva la gig*," she repeated, uttering his sentiments exactly. She sighed again.

After a very brief pause, they sighed in unison.

"In all my years, even with my heightened imagination, I never imagined this." He pointed first to her, then to himself.

She could see herself through his eyes, and she liked what she saw.

"Listen. They're beginning."

She listened. "What? I don't hear anything."

"Up there. Look up." He moved his head upward toward the sky. "Fireworks," he said.

She looked out at the horizon. A blank sky, but somewhere in the distance, she saw it, too - a spectacular display of fireworks. "Oh, yes, I can see them now, Sir Alfred Hitchcock," she said with great affection to the man seated next to her.

He got the movie reference and smiled. "*To Catch a Thief.*"

"Her hotel suite on the French Riviera on the couch with the diamond necklace."

"Grace Kelly," he said softly, referring to the star of the film. He reached for Valeska's hand.

"Cary Grant," she said lovingly, referring to Grace's co-star. She pressed Glick's fingers to her lips.

"You remember that scene?"

"A personal favorite," she replied. "Grace and Cary, the beautiful movie stars of yesteryear."

"Valeska and Glick, the beautiful people of today."

They sighed.

"It's a fact. So what if we need the ocean," he said. "You know, to get going." He winked at her, then looked at the water. "The rocking, up, down. The—"

"I get it, I get it," she said.

They held hands while imagining the fireworks and listening to the ocean waves beating against the shoreline.

Suddenly Valeska was hungry. Romance, schmomance, she thought. "I'm starving."

"We'll go to a restaurant. What do you feel like eating?"

She thought a second. "I'm craving lamb chops with mint jelly. No, maybe veal. I had fish last night. What do you think?"

Glick was listening but in a world of his own. "I'm thinking Grace Kelly."

Valeska was also in a world of her own. "And a nice baked potato with sour cream. You should have the salmon. You had meat twice this week."

"Ava Gardner," Glick went on.

"And for dessert, I think I'll have apple pie. I haven't had dessert in a long time. What about you?"

Still lost in lala land, he replied, "The Lana Turner parfait."

Valeska shot him a look, the kind of a look, when given to a man by the woman by his side, is known universally to be a grave error.

"I meant the Valeska Bernhart naturally."

"Naturally." Valeska smiled. "Maybe not the pie, maybe just a little strawberry ice cream. You?"

"Maybe chicken."

"Jello for dessert would be good. With a little fruit."

They continued their discussion about food for a while before actually standing up, getting in the car, and driving to a nearby restaurant.

18

AND...

Although no one had ever seen it, and it hadn't appeared on the front page of the National Enquirer...the buzz around West Palm Acres was that Valeska Bernhart and Glick Glickman indulged in activities of an intimate nature befitting a couple of their age. They neither denied or confirmed the gossip.

END

"Every wannabee and his brother want to be in a movie. I'm glad I'm on the other side of the camera."
—Tara Bombeck, Indie Film Director

"My medication is approximately the same as Goldberg's. So we split it in half. Saves money."
—Oscar Shapiro, resident at West Palm Acres

"We split the pills in half. If he dies, he dies."
—Harry Goldberg, resident at West Palm Acres

"Glick Glickman's been under the plastic surgery knife so many times, his face is in the back of his head."
—Harry Goldberg, resident at West Palm Acres

"Something's wrong with this mirror. I look terrible."
—Inky Krabb, stage actress

"My cousin Stanley once swallowed a lollipop whole. He became a psychiatrist and worked it out."
—Rocky Rage, stage actor

"When you're out of work in Hollywood, you can work on your tan."
—Ruby Valk, stage actress

"When I get shot on TV, they use ketchup. I bring my own bread and there it is. Lunch."
—Enzo Bordello, stage actor

"I ain't never seen a play, a movie, or read a book. My high school stressed woodworking and farming."
—Fat Cat (recently released from prison)
potential show biz financial backer

"In a flash, I'll bring p-zzazz back to Broadway. And it took God six days!"
—Glick Glickman, Broadway impresario

"As his gofer, I would do anything for Glick, even though he once said I had a profile like a demented carrot."
—Jane Smith, assistant to Glick Glickman

SUSAN SURMAN

After graduating from the School of Fine and Applied Arts (now College of Fine Arts), Boston University, as a theatre major, Boston-born actress turned author, SUSAN SURMAN lived and worked in London and Sydney (Gracie Luck / Susan Kramer) as an actress and playwright for over 23 years before returning to the States.

Acting highlights include London's West End, Edinburgh Fringe, Sydney Theatre Company (Sydney Opera House), BBC-radio, and numerous commercials. She has performed with such notables as Julia MacKenzie, Jacki Weaver, Robert Vaughn, Ed Bishop, Max Cullen, and Little Nell.

Writing credits include novels (*Afternoon Sun, Young Jiffo: The Australian Featherweight, Main Ingredient, West Palm Gig* (awarded), *Dancing at all the Weddings, Sacha: The Dog Who Made it to the Palace*, and *Max and Friends*); short stories (*Small Pickled Birds and Chocolate* (awarded), *Après Holiday*); stage (*In Between, George, The Nightgown, The Australian Featherweight*, and *West Palm Gig*).

Early credits: *George* was commissioned by the BBC TV, never aired. Thames TV hired Susan to write material for Tracy Ullman's first TV series. *You're Never Alone With Schizophrenia* (film) was optioned.

Awards: 2000 Porter Fleming 2nd place non-fiction category award: *Who Knew? Why Useless Information is so Useful*. Davidson County, NC Writers Guild 3rd place fiction: *Valeska*. Writer's Digest Honorable Mention in Plays Category: *In Between*, *Max and Friends*, *Valeska*, and *The Connection*.

Surman lives in North Carolina where she continues to write. She teaches classes part-time in writing and pronunciation in the English as a Second Language program at Forsyth Technical Community College. She has done presentations on "Creative Communication" at Wilkes Community College, Surry Community College, Forsyth Technical Community College, and Appalachian State University. She was Speech Director on *Amadeus* at Wake Forest University and taught a summer class at NC School of the Arts Drama School for incoming freshman.

susansurman@yahoo.com